I0603090

Wickedly Innocent

J.F. Lowe

Seduction and Sin Publishing

Wickedly Innocent

Wickedly Innocent
J.F. Lowe
Published by Seduction and Sin Publishing
Copyright @ 2021 J.F. Lowe
Edited by Bailey Macks
eBook ISBN: 978-0-6488818-8-9
Print IBSN: 978-0-6451020-3-1

All rights reserved. No part of this book may be repro-
duced, scanned, or distributed in any printed or electronic
form without permission. Please do not participate in or encourage piracy of copyrighted materials in violation of the
author's rights.

This is a work of fiction. Names, places, characters, and
incidents are the product of the author's imagination and are
fictitious. Any resemblance to actual persons, living or dead,
events or establishments is solely coincidental.

Warning: The contents of this book for a mature audience.

Prologue

"... Don't you even think of giving up, you can't leave me, I will not let you leave me...." Ashton blinked back the tears that threatened to fall as his hand tried to cover the bullet hole on his best friends bloodied chest. He looked at his face all twisted in agony. Tommy reached out weakly to grip Ashton's shirt. He tried to smile. He wanted to tell his best friend that he loved him like a brother, that it was all right, he would always watch over him, but he could not find enough strength to say what was on his mind. His breathing was failing. The pain was unbearable. He had never seen this coming, but again this world was never meant to be his. He looked up at the white ceiling as his life flashed before his eyes. He was grateful for every second of it. It was much more than he ever deserved. "Take care of her, love her. She'll need you". He smiled. He let go of his best friend, his brother, and closed his eyes....

Chapter 1

Dressed in little more than ill-fitting rags, a poor bastard of a fellow stumbled through the creaky front door of an equally haggard Lucky Sun motel. If he'd walked into any of the other establishments in this flyover town, he'd have been turned out on the spot, but he at least had enough of his wits about him to choose the dirtiest, most ragged option available.

As he stumbled his way to the front desk, he hoped that he'd stolen enough money. If not... well, it wouldn't be the first time he'd had to sleep out in the rain. What was one more night of suffering when he was so close to his goal? After a decade, there was only two hundred miles of open road between him and penance, vengeance, and a ruthless sense of cold-blooded satisfaction.

"Can I help you?" the attendant drawled without a single hint of surprise. Good to know that he wasn't particularly out of the ordinary as far as their usual clientele went. He would have looked up at her to get a better idea of how to handle the precarious interaction, but the last thing he wanted was to risk her recognizing his face.

"Just a room," he croaked, forcing down the burning sensation at the back of his throat. "One night, one occupant."

An impossibly long and neon-pink fingernail tapped the desk. The man dared to look up at the sound. The attendant wasn't staring in disgust or on the verge of laughing at his misfortune. No, there was something far worse lurking in her expression. There was pity.

He looked down at her finger and saw that she was tapping a list of rates that was taped to the cheap plastic surface of the desk. He wasn't exactly surprised to see that he could easily afford the indicated price.

With a shaking hand, he slid the crumpled bills across to her. She took them without counting, and a key clattered down in front of him.

He reached out to take the key, daring one more look up at her, searching for any glimpse of recognition. It was a long shot, but if she did recognize him, then it was better to know sooner than later.

But no, there was only a maternal concern that cut him even deeper. It might have been easier if she'd just recognized him for what he was, stared at him in horror, and rushed to call the police. Much easier.

"Thanks," he mumbled as he pocketed the key and lurched back out the way he'd come.

Outside, he quickly found the assigned room among the double-story block of cheap construction that made up the motel. Without meaning to, he took in the surroundings in an instant, a skill honed by both his years in prison and the even more dangerous years before that.

From the looks of things, both the rooms adjacent to his own were occupied. One had a beaten old pickup out from, exactly the sort of car he'd expect to find at a place like this. The other had a sleek, modern sports car instead, which in a twisted way, was also within his expectations. This was exactly the kind of place that someone from the upper crust would come to for illegal and scandalous activities. Perhaps not the most critical of information, but one never knew what might come in handy.

The key slid into the lock easily, and such was the man's exhaustion that he didn't even thoroughly examine the room for anything out of place. He couldn't even muster up the will to take a shower, despite never having needed one more in his life. As ratty and unappealing as the bed might be, it called out to him, and he obeyed.

It was different, his last free thoughts mused than prison. So very different. Here, the danger may not be any less, but at least nobody was leering over his shoulder, just waiting for him to make a mistake. No, his pursuers were much further away and much harder to escape. Here, he would sleep restfully for the first time in over a decade. At least, that is what he hoped with the last vestiges of consciousness.

Then, as the smothering pressure of sleep fell upon him, the writhing nightmares crept in. The loud crack of gunshots, so very much blood, and worst of all, the lifeless eyes. They had not left him alone in prison, so why would they leave him alone here?

No, he needed to complete his final mission before he was free of that. Then, and only then, could he have the rest that he craved but didn't deserve.

Chapter 2

Casey Anderson snapped awake, immediately slipping into the ritual that had kept her sane. First, eyes shut. Then, ten slow, steady breaths calmed her racing heart and gave herself time to dispel the night terrors that haunted her. It wasn't real. None of it was real. Believing that it was real would endanger the mission, and that was unacceptable.

She felt the urge to stretch but was far more disciplined than that. Instead, she ran through her memories from last night, piecing together the haziness and separating the very real sex from imagined torment.

Again, she suppressed an urge, this time to sigh. Finally confident that she was rooted in reality, she opened her eyes and took in the man lying at her side. He looked older now, which struck her as unusual. Normally, her marks tended to look younger while they slept, a combination of them being at their most vulnerable and them giving up the personas that they wore all the time while awake. This young man — and she very pointedly chose not to remember his name — conversely looked quite a bit older, from the broadness of his shoulders to the stubble on his chin. He looked like he was in his late twenties, but the way he'd been bursting with energy and constantly grinning last night had called to mind a restless teenager.

Casey didn't have it in her to shudder at the comparison. Her job was her job, and too much rode on her successes and failures to get wrapped up in what she actually thought about the men she seduced, drained of information, and left behind. Besides, the way he was draped nude across half the bed was enough to make her forget any potential misgivings. It was a good thing that the bed was so big, else he would have been halfway on top of her.

Which, she remembered with a faint aching warmth, wouldn't be the worst fate she could imagine. Their evening had been fun if a little overbearing. His eagerness had been charming up to a point, but the man really was like a puppy. What he lacked in experience and skill had mostly been made up for in enthusiasm.

But all of that was secondary to her real frustration: he was clean. One more name checked off the list, one more dead end on the grand mission to take down Ulrich. Better than nothing, she grudgingly acknowledged, but only slightly.

The agent rolled off the bed, silently landing on her feet and finally getting the kinks out of her neck. Slowly, she embraced the burn of her stretching routine, occasionally looking down at her slumbering lover with a thoughtful look in her eyes. The question wasn't whether to tell him her true purpose, never that. No, the only question that remained was whether she would leave him a note or not. Nothing more than a simple apology, maybe even thanking him for the night together. There was no advantage to it, not really, but she still felt terrible about leaving him completely in the dark. After all, he hadn't been working for Ulrich, so that had to count for something, right?

But, as always, pragmatism won out. That he wasn't working for a cunning, ruthless, evil criminal mastermind wasn't some great feat on his part. She would drift away without another word, never to see him ever again. It wasn't exactly likely that he'd be heartbroken, but this particular target had already shown a penchant for infatuation and quick attachments. His desperate desire to return certain flavorful favors last night could certainly attest to that. Always eager to please, and he'd probably take it exceptionally hard that she left.

There was no helping it, though. Casey's mission was far bigger than him and couldn't be put in jeopardy because some wide-eyed young man might develop an inferiority complex about his skills in bed because his lover vanished before he woke up.

He was a rather heavy sleeper, she mused as she finished up her stretches and set about gathering her scattered clothes. Not that it mattered much. If he had woken up, then she had a million, and one excuses ready to go. She always came prepared, which might have elicited a bemused grin if she hadn't already made the same joke a thousand times to herself.

As fully dressed as she was going to get, decked out in a slinky number that was great for catching the eyes of men with more lust than common sense, she took one last look at the snoring man and flicked a hand in what might have passed for a goodbye. It was her own little ritual, her way of separating herself from her targets after she'd taken them down. No sense in letting any feelings linger, and she found that adding a little motion to the thought went a long way.

Besides, she argued to herself that he deserved a better woman as she slipped out the back door. One without quite so many secrets, one that wasn't looking to take advantage of him. This was for the best, she reasoned. Perhaps it might even teach him to be a little more careful about who he trusted.

None of it mattered, not one bit. She didn't really care about him. That was something she'd figured out after a few years on the job. Before that point, everything had been hell, a constant state of flux where she had to swallow her heart every time she stepped into a bar at midnight or out of a house at dawn. Now, she knew better.

Down on the pre-dawn street, she glanced around, but nobody was awake yet. Once she was a few houses deeper in the sleepy neighborhood, she snapped her burner phone in half and tossed it in a conveniently located bin.

From there, it was a simple enough course. She just had to assume the hungover swaying of a girl on the walk of shame and make her way down to the parking garage that she'd left her car at. The odds of being watched were low but never zero.

Of course, such things were made quite a bit easier by the fact that she didn't have to fake the hangover.

At the entrance to the parking garage, she spied a bundle of rags that might have been a homeless person. The car with tinted windows across the street could be nothing, or it could be holding a full squad of lackeys, ready to burst out and end her investigation into Ulrich. Was that flash in the distance the rising sun or a camera? It may have sounded like a suspicious bunch of coincidences to a less experienced agent, but she knew better than anyone how the world was full of such warning signs every second of every day. The only difference between her and everyone else was that she noticed them, and now, after years of training, she was able to pick out the real threats from the imagined.

Ever vigilant, she mumbled to herself as she sauntered her way into the darkness, ready to sprint to safety at a moment's notice. Perhaps it was unnecessary to be so cautious, but then again, it was probably also unnecessary to add a little extra sway to her hips for the benefit of those greedy eyes that might have been watching her. With the line of work she'd chosen, it almost came easier to her than walking naturally.

She wound a roundabout path between the cars, more out of habit than any particular need to misdirect any potential tails. Her mind was far away, dwelling on memories that she would rather not focus on yet could not escape.

"Tommy," she murmured to herself without really meaning to. That, more than anything else, made her furtively glance around to see if anyone was watching. In some ways, having someone overhear her most private thoughts and fears was even more terrifying than the possibility that one of Ulrich's men might be tailing her with murderous intent.

Before she knew it, she was back at her car, a completely unassuming model. Better to deter any potential thieves that way, but that was more for their benefit than hers. She certainly wouldn't want to be the poor petty criminal that brought down a multi-million dollar investigation and the full weight of the law onto his head because he decided to break into the wrong car. Or her head, Casey added as an afterthought. God knows that she, of all people, knew just how dangerous women could be.

When she finally sat down in the driver's seat, after a cursory search for any signs of intrusion, Casey permitted herself a single sigh before cracking open the glovebox and pulling out the small terminal embedded there. Her secure link to her superiors was always the first thing she checked, but mission-critical updates only got her attention after she checked for any priority mentions of Ashton Malick.

Today, as always, there was absolutely no news about him. Figures.

With that out of the way, Casey was able to devote her full attention to filing her mission report. It was easy in the sense that there wasn't much to mention about the dead-end she had thoroughly, mercilessly, and deliciously explored, but hard in the sense that she now had to pick out a new trail to follow. There were so very many, and absolutely none had any potential worth noting. Old leads, old leads, and more old leads. That had been the state of things when she'd picked out her last target, and it was still the state of things now that she had one less lead to go down.

And yet, the total number of files in the directory had gone up. Frowning, she flicked through the names that she knew practically as well as she knew her own. Two more had been added since she'd last checked in. Dead ends that had been reopened on someone's hunch it seemed. Nothing particularly promising, but that was where the investigation was at: guts were just as valid as anything else, not because her division was prone to superstition, but because the actual evidence was really just that thin, and the brass was getting that antsy for results.

Casey took a look down at herself and almost considered hitting the road as she was. A skimpy little number was good for a lot of things in her line of work, but drifting down the highway beneath a scorching sun was not one of them. Sticking to the hot leather of her seats did not sound like her idea of fun.

Thus, she reached into the back seat, pulled out a bundle of unflattering sweats, and put on a more comfortable outfit. It was mildly amusing to imagine her lover from last night seeing her like this, but only mildly. Best to banish him from her mind and move on. There was only room enough in her heart to mourn one man.

Chapter 3

Several hundred miles away, feeling much refreshed but no less anxious, the lonesome wanderer shot down the highway, a black streak amid an endless wasteland of yellow and red. He kept looking in the rearview mirror, but there was still no pursuit. Not that he expected it quite yet, but years of honed paranoia wasn't easy to shake off.

The shitty pickup was every bit the old beast that he'd expected, but that was fine by him. When it came down to picking which car to steal that morning, half of his reasoning had come down to security. That nice sports car next door had looked mighty tempting, but who knows what kind of high-tech tracking a car like that has. Plus, it might have some newfangled fingerprint ID technology or something like that. On top of that, it wouldn't do to be flashy and easily recognizable, which the bright red speedster surely was.

The other half of the reasoning had been a bit more impulsive.

He'd woken up with a terrified start, barely able to distinguish reality from his dreams. Once he'd gotten his bearings and remembered that he was no longer in prison, it still took him a good half hour to calm down. That's when he heard the yelling on the other side of the wall.

At first, he'd thought it was just an extension of his own nightmares, a manifestation haunting him in his waking hours as well. It certainly wouldn't be the first time that such a thing had happened. In fact, the dire screaming and pounding on the walls sounded downright mellow compared to some of the sights and sounds that his guilty conscience had tormented him with.

But in time, he realized that this wasn't in his head at all. No, this was the rantings and ravings of a very real person, with a very thin wall separating them.

"You BITCH, is this how you repay everything I've done for you? You stupid slut, you utterly worthless piece of shit!"

Slamming on the wall punctuated nearly every word, but the more the newly awoken man listened, the more he was sure that there was only one person in the room. Unless it was the same sort of breakdown that he himself was prone to, it seemed the man was yelling at someone over the phone.

It was the room that should have the shitty pickup, he recalled from the parking spots out front. Not that it mattered all that much, but this did make him feel a bit better about stealing from the raving lunatic. If anything, it might give the guy a chance to calm down before he went and hurt someone, probably the person on the other end of the line, but with rage like that, it could be anyone that got in his way while en route.

There was no time to dawdle and take a shower, he decided as he lurched towards the door. He stank to high heavens, but at the same time, he wasn't exactly confident in the showers at a place like this. He might end up worse off than he'd gone in, and that was saying something.

Once outside, he crept his way over to the car in question. He waited and listened.

"What the fuck did you just say to me? What the FUCK did you just say to me?"

For whatever reason, the ranting and raving hadn't attracted the attention of anyone else quite yet. No, that wasn't quite right, the stranger remembered. His decade spent beneath the watchful eye of guards that delighted in stepping into any altercation had dulled him to the way things worked in the outside world. At a no-tell motel like this, you simply didn't stick your nose where it didn't belong, either because you were doing something just as illegal or because you simply didn't want to get shot.

And this would certainly qualify as a situation where one was liable to get shot. A thunderous slam shook the wall, which seemed as clear a sign as any to get this over and done with.

The stranger stepped up to the car, praying that his disreputable skills hadn't deteriorated too badly. After all, there hadn't been any occasions to break into cars while being behind bars.

As his trembling, grubby fingers worked, he tried very hard not to think about doing the right thing. It would be easy to intervene, it would be correct to intervene, and he practically had a moral obligation to intervene, but the last time he'd tried anything like that, everything had gone terribly, terribly wrong. So wrong that the last decade in captivity had only been the start of his punishment, at least as far as his thoughts on what he deserved were concerned. If you asked the law, it would have been for the rest of his natural life, and he wasn't so sure he disagreed with them on that. Really, the only point he quibbled on was whether he should be allowed to make some amends first.

But in a matter of moments, he was slipping into the pickup's seat and leaving behind all thoughts of playing the hero. Now was no time to ruin everything with the same crap that had ruined everything in the first place.

The truck rumbled to life beneath him. It felt good to be behind the wheel again after so very many years. And yet...

He had paused just a moment too long. When he looked in the rearview mirror and saw how that door shook with the barely-contained violence within, he was undone. Taking the guy's truck would delay him by a few hours, but this wasn't the kind of screaming fury that vanished after a couple hours. Maybe it would reduce to a simmer, and maybe he could fool everyone into thinking that it was totally gone, but it would still be there, and if it was anything like the stranger's own rage, it would only build with time, until it was a cold and ruthless creature that thought only of how to exact the bitterest and most devastating of revenges.

Leaving the truck running, he stepped down to the quickly-heating asphalt and rolled his sleeves up. This would only take a minute.

Chapter 4

Casey had been sitting in the booth for quite a while. She'd pulled into the diner's parking lot a good fifteen minutes ago. Since then, she'd spent the majority of her time on all the standard precautions. No tails had followed her into the lot, nobody had driven by suspiciously slowly, and she hadn't gotten any warnings on her terminal. In spite of it being mid-morning, the diner itself wasn't particularly busy at all. It being open twenty-four seven gave off the impression of being a popular haunt for night owls and truckers rather than the sort of brunch hotspot that would be bustling at this hour.

With a sigh, she perused the menu once more. It was impressive how she and her handler could arrange every single meeting at a different location, yet they all had the exact same homey atmosphere and grease-laden options. Not that she was complaining since a big ball of carbs and protein did sound like just what the doctor ordered for her borderline hangover. Nothing got the foul aftertaste of either tricking nice men or sleeping with bad men out of her mouth like a combination of bread, pork, eggs, and potatoes.

But should she indulge? Could she risk being more or less deadweight for the next several hours? Without warning, she was gripped by the memories of sitting with Tommy, her brother, at exactly such a diner, laughing at stupid stories as they sipped on coffee deep into the morning hours. When they were young kids, it had been a family tradition passed down from their parents. As they got older and went their separate ways, the quintessential diner experience had continued to represent cherished time that they could spend together on the rare occasion that their schedules aligned. Few things could bring tears to her well-trained features, but remembering those infrequent multi-hour diner sessions with her brother certainly numbered among them.

The kindly older waitress approached, exactly who one would expect to be working a greasy spoon, and just like that, Casey was back to her stone-cold, disinterested default expression. It is better to come off as a rude bitch than be taken advantage of because some surreptitious watchers saw an emotional weakness they could exploit.

"Want some more coffee, darling?" Given the fact that she was already reaching down to pour, it felt like a completely rhetorical question.

Casey muttered a quiet thanks, smiling tightly with the bare minimum of politeness. Any hope that it would encourage the woman to give her a little space and stop dropping by every few seconds was clearly in vain. In fact, given how the woman looked even more concerned at Casey's standoffishness, it may have had the exact opposite effect.

"Rough night, huh?" the waitress pressed.

Case glanced down at her clothes and wondered what exactly this woman was imagining. Then again, it was probably her expression that set the woman's maternal instincts into overdrive. Whatever it was, it certainly wasn't her problem.

"Something like that," she said, distinctly hoping the waitress would stroll away at the unsubtle dismissal and getting nothing of the sort. The older woman simply stood over her table, in no rush whatsoever, as she lightly held a notepad and pen.

Hunger was making her a little snappish, and Casey knew it. More out of spite than anything else, Casey gave the waitress her order, a hefty plate of bacon, eggs, hash browns, toast, and jam.

"You'll feel better after you eat," the woman said with a sympathetic quirk of her lips as she turned to languidly stroll away to the back of the restaurant.

Casey just nodded, surveying the room once again. It never hurt to be too careful. Still no sign of her contact, still nobody that looked out of place, still nothing for her to worry about. Hell, maybe she'd be able to actually wolf down this meal in peace.

The waitress had been right about one thing anyway. It had been a rough night, just probably not in the way that she imagined. If Casey stretched in just the right way, she could still feel a pleasant aching. At times like these, she had nothing to do but sit and wait for her handler, that she allowed herself to reflect on the more enviable aspects of her job.

She'd waited outside the house party until her team had all gotten in position. Staking out the exact movements of her target had been a multi-week affair, during which time she had little to do but study his tastes and habits. What kind of girls did he flirt with? What sort of alcohol did he prefer? What did he do in the bedroom once he thought he was alone and away from prying eyes? What she and her division did was an invasion of privacy, but the greater good was worth it. Bringing down Ulrich was worth it.

And then, when last night had finally come, it all came together. She crafted herself exactly to his tastes, enhancing the blush of her cheeks, picking the same shade of dark lipstick that he favored, and emphasizing her ass with a flattering dress that hugged her hips perfectly. He'd been ordering himself a drink when she walked in the door, his tousled hair and perpetual smile enough to endear him to her. And that moment when he finally swung around and saw her... it still gave her shivers.

She'd barely even had to feign disinterest as he made a beeline for her. It was almost enough to make her feel bad for his naivete. Almost.

Within two minutes, she had him following her around like a puppy, waiting on her hand and foot.

Within twenty minutes, she had him spilling his deepest, darkest secrets. Unfortunately, they leaned far more towards "embarrassing childhood stories" rather than "suspicious and potentially incriminating evidence of criminal conspiracy."

She didn't take him at his word, obviously. Really, she was just there to keep him occupied while her team searched his place and checked for anything out of the ordinary. It only took them slightly longer to corroborate his story and give the all-clear.

The all-clear so far, as it was. Her mission parameters allowed no deviation. Seduce the target, sleep with them, extract information when they're at their most vulnerable. All her investigation so far had proved was that she didn't need to keep a hand on her hidden weapon during the foreplay, both metaphorical and literal.

And so, within two hours, she had her target hot and heavy out behind the house. A nip here, a kiss there, and he was desperate enough to do anything she wanted. Casey was compelled, but her capacity to bring men to their knees was second only to her discipline. Unlike them, she was never ruled by her base desires.

But even a woman with perfect discipline was allowed to fidget once in a while, and so Casey crossed her legs to delight in remembered sensations for a little while longer.

Finally, out of the corner of her eye, she spied her contact, her handler, and her moderately friendly acquaintance entering the diner, with the bell tinkling as the door swung open.

Carlisle was a drab, uninspiring man that took great care to appear as nothing more than a tedious office drone. He wore the same bland colors every day, dressed in nothing more adventurous than an old and well-worn suit, and was perpetually frowning in mild disapproval. He was a good man, but there was something about him today that immediately struck Casey as off.

He scanned the room for a moment, quite the expert when it came to looking like a frightened deer. She knew from experience that such a description was only partially accurate for the man. While he was a bit more squeamish and soft-hearted than most in the division, he was still a consummate professional.

The moment he spotted her, he headed right over to the booth and plopped himself down across from her. Casey thought she detected a flicker of something on his face, but it passed too quickly to be sure.

"How's the coffee here?" he muttered as he fiddled with his briefcase.

"Good," Casey lazily said back. "Gonna order?"

He checked his watch, always in a rush. "Afraid not, I have to get reports from... well, you know."

Indeed she did know. Best not to talk about anything but matters of immediate and critical importance. Less of a chance of eavesdropping that way.

The moment stretched out, and Casey's immediate instinct that the waitress would be back any second to take his order was proven to be wrong. The moment kept right on stretching, and from the way Carlisle wasn't quite meeting her eyes, she knew something was wrong.

"What is it?" she asked tersely.

"It's noth—" The excuse died on his lips as he finally looked up at her. He glanced down at his watch, surely wondering how many precious seconds it would cost for another pregnant pause. "Anything to report from last night?" he asked at last.

"Only what was in the report. Dead end," Casey said quickly and quietly. She leaned forward, which had the intended effect of making her loom over Carlisle. "Is it Malick?"

He swallowed but valiantly met her stare. "Yes," he very nearly whispered. "He broke out four days ago."

Casey looked down to see that one hand was still around the mug's handle. If she squeezed any harder, she might just snap it off completely. With slow, laborious intent, she relaxed her fingers and folded her hands in front of her. When she finally had at least a modicum of control over her emotions, she stared Carlisle down once again. "And why didn't you tell me in my last update?"

Carlisle eyed her more warily this time but more confidently as well. It was the way one looked at a wild animal that they held a healthy amount of respect for. Then, he snorted. Snorted!

"It would be rather stupid of me to tell you a thing like that anywhere but in person. The last thing we need is you gallivanting off to get your revenge and leaving all of us in the lurch. And don't even bother trying to deny it, you know that's exactly what you'd do."

Casey clenched her jaw shut, knowing that he was right. Granted, it wouldn't have mattered all that much if she'd abandoned this dead-end of an investigation, but it was the principle of the thing.

"Where is he now?" she murmured through gritted teeth, but her mind was already racing. Four days meant that he could only have gotten so far away. If it was an orchestrated breakout and he had assistance, then he could already be on a plane and headed anywhere, but if not... if the man had been working under his own power and with limited means, then the search radius was still small. There was still time to catch him.

Carlisle watched her run through the calculations with worry that almost reached her heart.

But no, there was no room for any of that now. She may have failed to get her revenge last time, but fate was giving her a second chance. Ashton Malick wouldn't get away with anything so simple and easy as a life sentence in prison this time around. By the end of this chase, no matter how long it took, one of them would end up six feet under. This she swore.

There was nothing more to say. Casey stood up, not quite sure what to say to her mentor, but also ready to leave without saying anything at all if inspiration failed to strike. She tossed down more than enough to cover the meal she'd abandoned before it had even arrived.

"What are you going to do?" he asked.

That, she knew how to reply to. It was nice of him to make this easy for her.

"Exactly what I was trained to do. Nothing more, nothing less." And with that, Casey Anderson left him behind to embark on the quest for vengeance that had eluded her for so very long.

But, right as she reached the door, she heard the waitress bring her heaping platter of food to the table. She hesitated for a single moment, watching Carlisle's slumped shoulders as he politely asked the waitress to bring a to-go box. The man wouldn't eat it himself, not with his blood pressure. It would be for his kids. They'd been through this a hundred times before, at a hundred different diners, but this time, it hit Casey differently.

Before, it had been a reminder of what she'd lost. No more family for her to share such things with. No parents to worry like Carlisle did. No brother to thoughtfully share greasy breakfasts with.

Now, it came with the surety that nobody else would have to suffer like she had. Once this was done, Ashton Malick would never destroy another family again.

Chapter 5

With a smoldering gaze born of more than just animal lust, Casey sat in the most upscale bar she'd graced in the last few months. Located on the ground floor of a flashy hotel, it was exactly the kind of place where she expected to find the swaggering sorts that filled the lower rungs of Ulrich's criminal organization. It was exactly the sort of place she expected Malick to go once for aid.

Her appearance, as always, was virtually unrecognizable when compared to how she'd looked both this morning and the previous night. Hair cut, curled, and dyed into a vibrant red, shoulders covered and clung to by a dress that was provocatively conservative. Cheeks sculpted to look narrower by the miracle of modern makeup, she surveyed her hunting ground and waited for her prey.

The passing hours had done nothing to quell Casey Anderson's rage. Every moment, Malick had a chance to slip further and further away, but all she could do was lie in wait. Her other team members handled the search and cooperation with local authorities, but her specialization forced her to stick to the sidelines. However, that hardly meant that she had to be useless. Every good huntress knew that laying the proper groundwork was just as important as the chase itself. As such, she had set about establishing herself to the patrons that were slowly beginning to fill the swanky bar.

A younger businessman kept trying to catch her eye from several seats down, but he wasn't confident enough to buy her a drink yet. The way he fidgeted and kept shifting in his seat to catch her eye spoke to a combination of youthful confidence and inexperience that she very much did not want to deal with right now, and not only because of the man she'd seduced and abandoned last night. Besides, it was often best to let the indecisive sort moon over her for as long as possible, if only because it forced everyone around to pay attention to her as well.

She wasn't completely cold to him, though. From time to time, she flashed a longing look in his direction, always angled just enough that he couldn't quite tell if he was looking at him or over his shoulder. Each time, he tensed, and he gripped the bar as though to push himself up to his feet, but each time, his courage fled. A small part of her wanted to tell him to get the hell out of here, that he wasn't going to like the sort of clientele that frequented this place after dark, but as always, it was only a small part. Tonight, with Malick so near she could taste his vile filth, it was even smaller.

Of course, Casey didn't neglect the rest of the bar either. She fluttered her eyelashes at the bursting-with-bravado toughs that either worked for Ulrich on the street level or aspired to work for him. She quirked an eyebrow at the bartender, uncrossed and recrossed her legs to offer the impression of impropriety to the pair of quiet young laborers that were just here for the cheap drinks, and even brushed her lip against her teeth to shock an older woman that kept sending curious glances her way.

The last was the most amusing, not because Casey had any particular issue with seducing the fairer sex, but because the woman was equal parts scandalized and intrigued. Such diversions were what made the emotionally fraught wait bearable.

But then the door opened, and he walked in. Not Ashton Malick, not for sure, but a near enough resemblance that every one of her instincts screamed that it might be her target in disguise. Short dark hair and even darker eyes, broad shoulders held with self-confidence that infuriated her, nondescript, generic clothes meant to blend in with any latenight crowd... it looked the spitting image of Malick, but even so, she knew that wasn't enough.

Moreover, what she remembered of her nemesis was ten years out of date. Sure, she'd seen updated pictures from his time in prison, but those couldn't really convey how the man would look once he was free. There was a world of difference between that slumping, broken shell of a man and the swaggering paragon of self-assurance that was striding towards the bar.

Normally, it was trivial enough to keep up her calm persona and react with utter indifference, but not this time. This time, she had to practice every little trick in the book to keep her breathing under control, to prevent her from shaking with a combination of rage and terror. It was all she could do to keep a bored look on her face as she looked straight ahead and ignored his presence at her elbow.

"The usual," he rumbled with a voice that she intimately knew, from the bottom of her heart, to not be Malick's. "Big U's got us working nonstop, the slavedriver."

Casey breathed out slowly, steadily, recalculating and falling back into comfortable patterns. This wasn't Malick. Disappointing, but she was a patient woman. More annoying was the fact that he was so blatant about his ties to Ulrich. If he'd been even remotely ambiguous about the whole thing, then she could just feign ignorance and let it slide, continuing to wait for her true prey.

But he hadn't been ambiguous. He'd name-dropped the bastard, and now she had an obligation to hunt him down. The mission didn't end just because her personal vendetta was finally close to resolution.

And so she knew, from the bottom of her heart, that she had an obligation to seduce this bastard, drain him of any pertinent info, and deliver a judgment to her team on whether he should be taken in for further interrogation.

Chapter 6

Casey turned to face her target with a suppressed sigh, subtly pushing out her chest just enough to make a difference. His face lit up with unmistakable glee, splitting his mouth wide in a leering smile. This would be easy.

"Don't think I've seen you around here before," he murmured as he looked her up and down. His raking gaze felt dirty, but Casey had been objectified harder by more dangerous men than this.

"No, I'm new in town," she drawled, affecting an accent that struck her fancy. "I figured it was a good idea to meet the people worth knowing around here. You qualify?"

He squinted at her, reaching out to take beer the bartender had just delivered. Casey made a quick course correction, deciding that it would likely be better to stick to short, sweet answers. This was the kind of man that was liable to get annoyed at women that spoke too much.

"Yeah, I think I'm someone you should get to know." Once again, and making sure that she saw exactly what he was doing, he pointedly looked down, lingering on her breasts, then on her crotch.

This had always been the hardest part of her job. It was easy enough to play along in bed and easier still to cling to a man's arm and escort him to wherever he wanted to have his fun, but to sit there in front of a disgusting man and force yourself to flirt was simply a pain in the ass. She had to force herself to look for whatever tiny fragment of appeal that these men might have, for they always seemed to know if your flirting was a complete fabrication. There always had to be some kernel of truth to your compliments, else they might suspect that something was wrong.

Once they were fucking, things would be different, though. She imagined this braggart on his back, sweating and huffing as she rode him straight to completion. It would be nice to dig her fingers into his shoulders, to see him feel a touch of pain. It was almost shocking how pliable this kind of guy was once you got behind closed doors. All that bluster vanished, replaced with a vulnerability and willingness to be guided that stemmed from a deep terror that the woman might criticize their skills, either in public or private. Sure, sometimes they lashed out and tried to take control of the coupling, but that was easy enough to manipulate once you got the hang of it, and Casey definitely had the hang of it by now.

His hand, as expected, drifted over to settle on her knee. The huntress forced herself to feel a tiny flutter of excitement, which she then forced to show on her cheeks.

"Excited, are we?" she whispered breathlessly. "And here I thought you were a gentleman."

He grinned at that, an awkward, lopsided expression on his tanned face. "An excited gentleman, I guess you could call me. How much is it for a ride?"

This was the second hardest thing at her job: not laughing at the men who mistook her for a prostitute. It was almost sad the way they thought that the only way a woman might give them attention was if she had ulterior motives. Which, she supposed, wasn't exactly inaccurate in her case, a fact that only made the urge to snort stronger.

But, as she had long since learned, it was usually easier to go along with their preconceived notions than to jeopardize the whole thing by feigning outrage.

"Two fifty," she said without hesitation. Given the glitz and glamor of the location, that struck her as a reasonable starting point.

He blanched at that but quickly regained control of his expression. "That's... for everything?"

She grinned at that, letting some of her genuine humor seep through. "No, that's just for the ride. No kissing, mouths, or otherwise. Maybe some hand action to warm you up, if you'd like."

The plan was quickly taking form in her head. Every assignment was different, with some requiring a bit of groundwork before the screwing in order to prime the target and others being best handled with a single surprise attack when they're completely vulnerable. This one... probably fell into the latter category, Casey decided. Best to lull him into a false sense of security, then interrogate him about Ulrich while cum was still dribbling from his cock.

"Okay," he muttered, obviously doing some mental math to fit this into his budget. His grip tightened on her knee, and she tried very hard to imagine that he had some skill with women in bed. It was unlikely, but a girl could dream. "Okay! You want to get out of here?"

Casey took a long moment to look around the room, ostensibly to think about his answer, but actually to make sure nobody was watching with what she would consider excessive attention.

"I suppose so. We can take a room upstairs if you want."

His brow furrowed at that. "And I'm guessing I'd have to pay for that?"

She flashed him a smile that was only slightly predatory. "Good guess."

"No, I've got a place," he mumbled as he shifted his hand up to take her wrist. The pull as he rose was insistent but not painful. Not yet.

As expected, he was the possessive sort, imagining that if he wasn't holding onto a girl at all times, then someone else would come and steal her away. Probably because he's the kind of guy that would enviously watch and wait for exactly such an opportunity to steal a pretty girl away from someone else. At least that made her job easy.

Casey rose to her feet, feigning a brief stumble that allowed her to squeeze up against her target, pressing against his arm and holding onto him for support.

"So what did you say your name was, sugar?" she asked, right into his ear. In her experience, she always had the most luck when ambushing guys like this. As it turns out, it's much harder to lie with a straight face when a girl is whispering into your ear.

"Charlie," he said with a nervous swallow. She was so very close as she looked up at his profile. She watched his Adam's apple move, allowing that perhaps this wouldn't be the worst roll in the hay that she'd ever had.

"I like that name," she whispered, reaching up on her tiptoes to nip at his ear. "Do you want to know my name?"

He nodded jerkily, still standing beside the bar, paralyzed by the teasing of a government operative posing as an escort.

"You'll have to earn it," she breathed, and just like that, tugged him along by the hand to the exit. He was going to have to lead the way to wherever they were going, but she could keep him off-balance until they got outside.

He stumbled along behind her, struggling to regain his bravado. He did manage it, though, puffing his chest out and rushing ahead to take charge and walk as her equal. That suited Casey just fine, seeing as it let her lean against him and wrap herself around his admittedly muscular arm.

It was always funny watching tanned men blush as she pushed her breasts up against them. You could always tell the exact moment when they realized that she wasn't wearing a bra.

"So is your place nice?" she asked as they reached the exit and stepped out into the encroaching twilight.

He looked up and down the street, vigilant but not particularly subtle about it.

"Worried about your girlfriend seeing us?" she teased.

"Don't have one," he said under his breath, pulling her down the street towards a block of apartments.

Noted. It was a tiny fact, barely worth learning, but every little bit went in the report. It was that sort of preparation and attention to detail that meant she knew exactly where they were going. There was a large block of properties with ties to Ulrich around here, including a selection of rooms that his lackeys used as safe houses and properties. Her division had theorized that they were granted out based on loyalty and taken away just as quickly for failures, so perhaps she would be able to learn some concrete info if she actually got inside.

At her side, Charlie was finally satisfied that nobody was watching and turned his attention to the beautiful woman at his side. Within moments, he pulled out of her affectionate partial embrace and wrapped an arm around her, hugging her close and making it hard to walk. Naturally, he began to grope her breast.

"Out here in public? That's very adventurous of you," she murmured, wondering if she should reach down to tease him a little bit in turn. It could set him aflame, but at the same time, it wouldn't do to anger him if he thought himself in control now. Wouldn't want him to flinch and lash out because he was terrified that one of his mates or rivals might have seen him in a moment of weakness. No, he wouldn't want that at all.

Which is exactly why she reached down and caressed his crotch for a fraction of a second, not nearly long enough for a definitive accusation of intentional fondling, but more than long enough for her to feel out his exact proportions and level of excitement.

His package was... acceptable. However, far more enticing was the way he shuddered and jumped in response, staring straight ahead and not daring to meet her gaze. Seemed that he was a little less confident and familiar with the affections of women than it might seem. It was almost enough to make her think of him as a poor guy.

"I'm gonna fuck you so hard," he whispered harshly, reaching down to grab her ass but still facing straight ahead. Seems he wanted to reclaim control of the dynamic but didn't have the courage to actually look a handsy prostitute in the eyes.

Then, oddly enough, they turned down an alley. If her mental map of the area was correct — and it most certainly was — then this was a detour that only made the journey longer. What had been the onset of night on the well-lit street turned into a dark gray corridor that set every one of her nerves on edge.

She laughed nervously, which was only partially feigned. This would be a wonderful place for an ambush, but she didn't get the impression that she'd been made. Perhaps this was an entirely different scenario, where he was merely arranging for her to be hurt because she's a woman and not because she's an agent on his boss's trail. That was enough to make her reach down and finger the small pistol tucked into her garter belt.

But then she caught a glimpse of his face in the sporadic lighting. There was a self-satisfied grin there, the kind she'd seen a hundred times before. It was nothing so thrilling or dangerous as the cold nervousness of men preparing to do serious harm but the sadistic menace of men who enjoyed making women think they were in danger. Minute by minute, she was growing more and more secure in her assessment of his character and threat level: impotent, hateful, cowardly, miserable, self-loathing. Exactly the kind of guy that she loved bringing to justice.

Right when she was beginning to feel confident in her strategy and the direction the night would take, the world exploded into loud, clanging chaos.

Casey sprang backward and away from the commotion, driven by pure adrenaline and reflex. She crouched, reduced her profile, and struggled to make sense of what she saw and heard.

As best she could tell, someone had launched a surprise attack on them. Throwing an empty trash can had been involved, judging by the cacophony of hollow metal banging. Two figures were engaged in a brawl, one of which looked to be Charlie. The other... looked more like a feral animal than anything else.

It was a dilemma of the most frustrating kind. Was it just a resident of the alley that was furious at being interrupted? Someone with serious mental problems? Should she step in and help her target? If so, should she show her skills and defuse the situation easily or feign complete inexperience and endanger everyone involved? To abandon the mission or not?

She reached down to finger her tiny sidearm once more, creeping closer to get a better feel for who was advantaged. One was down on the ground, the other on top of them. A dangerous situation, ripe for permanent damage.

Casey breathed in and began to pull her gun but then reconsidered. A new possibility presented itself.

"Don't hurt him!" she screeched with as much grating shrillness as she could muster. "Stop fighting!"

That was enough to freeze the scene. The man on top was definitely the feral stranger, which meant that Charlie was under him.

"Let me help him!" she blubbered, rushing forward with no regard for tactics or strategy.

The plan was simple enough and even borderline romantic. Rush to Charlie's rescue, escort him back to his room, then show a tender heart and nurse some of his injuries. It was the ideal turn of events, but it all hinged on whether she was able to get through to his attacker.

It was a hunch, and perhaps nothing more than that, but something about that dirty, rangy man made her think that he wasn't quite as unhinged as he first seemed.

The moment stretched out as he turned to stare at her. By now, her vision had acclimated to the darkness. Black, terrible eyes stared back at her from under a tangled snarl of lanky black hair. His whole body was tense and ready to spring into action. Beneath him, Charlie was groaning, clearly disoriented, but also clearly not dead yet. It was a cruel, callous calculation, but she didn't need him alive, she just needed him alive long enough to give her answers.

Raising his hands to an unthreatening posture, the attacker stepped back from his victim, maintaining eye contact with Casey, as though she was the wild animal and he was trying to placate her.

She frowned internally, careful not to break the illusion of her emotional, womanly display of emotion. Men were so much easier to trick when you let them believe what they wanted about how women behaved.

There was something off about the man, something she couldn't quite place.

"Let me take him to get help," she pleaded, taking a shaky step forward. "He needs medical help."

The attacker opened his mouth, then closed it. His lips tightened in a grim line as he looked down at Charlie.

She didn't want to shoot him for a number of reasons, ranging from not wanting to bring the authorities to a more general aversion regarding ending a man's life, but if it came down to it, she was ready. In one smooth motion, she could pull her pistol and put three bullets in him before he closed the distance.

But he just stepped back one more time, a clear enough indicator that she could go help her fallen man.

Maybe this had all just been a big misunderstanding then? The thought very nearly made her laugh aloud without any humor whatsoever. When you got down to it, maybe everything about this evening came down to misunderstandings, first with Charlie misunderstanding her, then this attacker not understanding who was invading his alley, then with the attacker not understanding Casey's angle.

Slowly, she stepped forward and kneeled down at Charlie's side, measuring his pulse, but never taking her eyes off the attacker, nor her hand from the gun-bearing thigh.

"You his woman?" a voice rasped. It took her a disorienting moment to realize it came from the attacker.

She flicked a glance down to see if Charlie was conscious enough to warrant playing coy. "Something like that. I just need to get him to safety."

"Why?"

She watched him carefully, weighing which approach would work best on a man like him. As it turns out, spending your whole life perfecting the art of seducing dangerous criminals didn't leave one with a ton of experience when it came to handling wild men that looked like they'd just stumbled in from the wilderness.

"Because he needs help," she said slowly, enunciating every word. "I'm guessing you don't mean to kill him since you didn't finish the job when you could have."

He just kept staring at her, emotion utterly absent from his face. Casey couldn't help but wonder if this is what her victims felt like when they looked her in the face after she'd let the facade fall away.

It would have to be enough. She crouched down beside Charlie, praying that he had enough of his faculties left to stand partially under his own power. Carrying him may have been in her power, but doing so while still keeping a hand free to pull her gun certainly wasn't.

And then the attacker was on the other side of Charlie, kneeling to help her lift. Within moments, the pair were standing, supporting the injured man and only letting his feet slightly drag on the ground.

An unexpected and concerning turn of events, but Casey was nothing if not adaptable to rapidly changing circumstances. With a few grunts, they went down the alley, back the way they'd come. She'd just have to hope that the attacker wasn't plotting some other assault down the line, that he didn't ask why they were turning around, and that Charlie didn't wake and ask how she possibly knew where his house was.

In the back of her mind, doubt was beginning to take root. At first glance, this man looked nothing like Ashton Malick. Gone was the proud bearing, gone were the laughing, insidious eyes, and gone was every bit of handsomeness that he'd once clung to in his neverending vanity. Ashton Malick had been nothing short of beautiful, which had only made her infatuation and his subsequent betrayal all the more brutal.

This man, this poor bastard of a fellow, looked nothing like Malick. And yet...

Chapter 7

As Ashton Malick lugged a little over half the guy's weight, two distinct problems demanded all of his concentration. First, he needed to get answers out of this low-life sack of shit by any means necessary. No matter what it took, no matter how dirty his hands had to get, he would wring names from this pile of human filth.

Second... well, the second problem was giving him quite a bit more trouble. He needed to get rid of the man's companion, but there were a couple snags in the way, not the least of which being that she was currently rather indispensable. As much as Ashton might want to beat the answers out of this bastard on the spot, someone would stumble onto them sooner or later. No, best handle it in a safe, secure location where he could take all the time he needed.

"His place is this way," she muttered under her breath, broadly gesturing with one hand. Malick was more than happy to let her lead the way, or at least as much as one could manage to lead the way while carrying half a man.

There was also the matter of the woman's relationship with Charlie. He knew, by every bone in his body and every bit of experience he'd mustered over the years, that she looked like she was a bit of hired companionship, but that wasn't the kind of thing that someone just threw out there without warning. Telling her to get lost and that he'd take it from here would surely work if she was being paid by the hour, but if she was actually his partner and just chose to dress like that of her own volition...

But he wasn't saying that she looked like a whore. He wanted to be very clear about that, as he spoke to nobody but the voice in his head that had kept him mostly sane for the last decade. She looked very fine and nice and pleasant, and even if she did look like a prostitute, then who cares? Prostitutes are people too, and deserving of every bit of respect he could muster.

"Get a fucking grip, Ashton," he mumbled. He could let his brain careen down useless tangents once today was over, when he was lying on another shitty motel bed, paid for with more stolen money, and getting the last bit of rest he needed before—

He cut that line of thinking off, shifting his weight slightly to carry his insensate enemy a little easier. Getting ahead of himself wouldn't do anyone any good. Had to get some leads first, then he could continue.

He stole a glance at the woman on the other side of Charlie. For just an instant, it looked like she was watching him intently, but then her face smoothed into polite disinterest, which, he decided, was a very odd expression for their circumstances.

"So... you do this often?" he asked, almost casually.

It was a feeble attempt at humor, and judging by her bland reaction, not of a sort that appealed to her.

"Oh yeah, alllllll the time," she deadpanned, shifting her stance to adjust the weight on her shoulder. It was probably just Ashton's imagination, but it sure felt like she was forcing to take a little bit more of the load.

Right, different tack then. They trudged on for a few moments of silence amidst a pathway that was less than a road but more than an alley. Not a soul was in sight to mark their progress.

"So uh... this your boyfriend?"

There, that seemed like a reasonably innocuous question to get the subject out in the open. Granted, he just had to hope that his last dumb comment hadn't soured her for answers completely, but at least it was a start.

Ashton fought the urge to look over and read her expression as she failed to reply.

"Something like that," she said at last.

Well, that didn't clear things up much.

"Like... your boyfriend for the rest of an hour, and then you're strangers again?" Even as the words left his lips, he marveled at their foolishness. If that's all it was, then why the hell was she carrying his unconscious ass down the street? Any prostitute would have just left him on the filthy pavement and walked away.

"A few hours tonight, a few hours tomorrow, a few hours yesterday. Not exactly interested in a lucrative lover dying in the street," she added at the end as if to show that she could read his thoughts.

"Makes sense," he grumbled as they turned a corner.

Charlie shuddered and moaned. The pair paused to see if he was truly rousing, but the moment passed, and he was once again dead weight. Ashton wasn't particularly bothered by the possibility of the man having permanent brain damage from his injuries, not as long as he could be lucid enough to answer a question or three before his wits turned to mush.

That inevitably led him to wonder exactly how he was going to extract the information he needed. No matter what he'd known before spending a decade among hardened killers and conniving bastards, those ten years had taught him more than any man should know about how to coerce info. Most of that had come via hearsay and stories, but a small fraction had been personally experienced or witnessed.

He shivered at the memories but was promptly interrupted by the escort.

"I hope you don't have the wrong idea about this."

He glanced over at her, which was rather easy with Charlie's head sagging so low. "Beg your pardon?"

"I hope you don't think you're gonna get a freebie out of this," she said, pointedly refusing to meet his gaze until she was good and ready. When she finally did turn to punctuate her statement, there was a hardness to her stare that stirred something deep inside Ashton. Whether it was a long-forgotten memory or something more primal, he could not say.

After a moment, he finally processed what she'd said.

"No, obviously not. Why would I expect you to gratefully get down on your knees because I knocked out your last client and somewhat forced you to carry him down half a dozen blocks?"

She was silent for a time, long enough that he thought no response was forthcoming.

"So your preference is a girl down on her knees. Noted."

That time, he was quite sure that there was a heavy edge of sarcasm. Not that he was particularly surprised to find that a jaded escort might have the same sense of humor as a man as broken as himself.

But she wasn't done quite yet. The escort cleared her throat.

"So why exactly are you helping this guy that you just beat the shit out of back to his place? You gonna tell me this was all some friendly misunderstanding?"

It was a peculiar position to be in, and Ashton grunted unnecessarily from the exertion just to give himself a moment to think. He obviously couldn't tell the truth... or could he?

She was from around here, and her clients were clearly of a certain caliber. It wouldn't shock her to know that he was going to do some more harm to the bastard. After all, that was just the way things worked around here.

"He's got something that belongs to me," he said at last, which was arguably true, albeit in an exceptionally roundabout way. After all, if someone possessed information that would lead to one's freedom, then couldn't it be argued that they owned something of yours?

Out of the corner of his eye, he could spy a frown on her face. For a moment, it felt like she was going to press and continue her questioning, but nothing came.

And then, with one more turn, they found themselves on the street where their destination lay. Neither said anything as they moved through the alternating pattern of dilapidated, abandoned old shops and bleak blocks of apartments. It was a dangerous place, which Ashton knew not only from his last few hours of prowling but from when he'd visited the area years and years ago. If anything, it had only gotten worse since Ulrich had risen in the organization.

Chapter 8

Casey stood in the elevator, trying to keep her mind as clear as possible. It wouldn't do to look too suspicious or too thoughtful, not if she wanted to maintain her cover as not just an escort, but a woman who sold her time, services, and body to the kind of people that disliked questions. Thus, she did not focus upon the details of her plan or the escape routes that she'd memorized. Instead, she occupied herself with the mundane and mildly engaging question of whether she'd ever taken a stranger elevator ride than this.

Sure, she'd dealt with clients that liked a bit of friskiness in the tantalizing, minorly dangerous context that the door might open at any time. She'd even brought men all the way to the edge and beyond on particularly long elevator rides, but that was more a testament to their excitement and lack of control than her own expertise. Hell, one time, she'd even had her way with two men in an elevator that had broken down, a memory that still gave her a slight shudder now and then.

However, she was quite sure that she'd never been in an elevator where she and the man she hated most in the entire world were propping up a man that had ostensibly been her former client. That was certainly a new one.

On the walk over, she'd worried a bit about how she might ultimately handle the question of her history with Charlie. If the guy did wake up, then him claiming not to know who she was might be a problem. Or rather, it would have been a problem if he hadn't taken such a nasty hit to the head. The fact that he hadn't woken up by now spoke to some serious damage that would easily explain away any inconsistencies in her story.

As if in response to her thoughts, Charlie started, and the man that she was quite sure was Ashton Malick caught his arm. However, the man roused no further than that, easily settling back into the corner of the elevator. After a moment, Ashton's wariness gave way to fatigued resignation once more.

The fact that her true quarry was clearly exhausted should have made Casey feel better, but she couldn't help the niggling feeling in the back of her mind that perhaps he was simply faking it. Even if he wasn't, he was still a slippery son of a bitch that she couldn't afford to underestimate.

Ashton sighed heavily but did nothing further. Slowly, Casey relaxed and pulled her fingers away from her concealed sidearm. She needed to calm down, especially if her tentative plan was to come to fruition.

Glancing up, she couldn't help but marvel at how slowly the elevator was moving. Long seconds passed between each floor, granting both a growing sense of relief that nobody had tried to get on thus far and an impending sense of doom that someone might do it right before they reached their goal.

She would need to make her decision quickly. She was almost entirely sure the man was Asthon, but only almost. There was a chance, no matter how minute, that she was mistaken. In that case, she could not let this man maim or kill Charlie, not before she interrogated him. In that sense, her course was clear: if she was unable to verify that the man was indeed Ashton Malick, then she needed to stop things before they went too far.

Ding.

At last, the eighteenth floor and their destination. Hopefully, her intelligence was correct.

Ashton sighed heavily once more, flicking her an unreadable look before bending his knees to pick up his half of Charlie's weight. Casey followed suit, but just like before, made sure that Ashton was bearing the lion's share. It wasn't purely a matter of spite, she told herself, but a tactically valid means of putting her potential opponent at a disadvantage while simultaneously making it easier for her to draw.

The dour hallway buzzed with unpleasant fluorescent lights, casting everything in a sickly mix of shadows. It was exactly the kind of depressingly malicious place that she would have expected Ulrich to house his lowly peons.

Fortunately, the door in question was relatively near the elevator.

As they drew up to it, Ashton mumbled something to himself and guided Charlie up to the wall, where he awkwardly relieved himself of the weight. The insensate criminal slumped face-first against the ugly plaster, which would certainly hurt once he woke up. For her part, Casey managed to extricate herself with ease, narrowly avoiding being pulled down into an undignified heap.

Her every nerve was alert for an attack, but it seemed that Ashton hadn't been trying to put her off-balance, at least not for any explicitly dangerous purpose. Rather, he was hunched over the lock, working quickly at opening the door. Trying to distract her then?

Casey leaned against the wall, watching his back and thinking. He was picking the lock, that much was obvious. The question was why he didn't want her to know that. Perhaps he believed that he was convincingly pulling off the illusion that he was a friend of this man and that he had a perfectly good reason to be in the apartment, such as a gifted key?

Rather foolish of Ashton, she'd thought him a hair smarter than that.

"Having trouble with the key?" she called out, curious to see how he might respond. It felt like a normal enough question for an insouciant prostitute that had just been forced to drag half of a couple hundred pounds.

"No, I'm obviously picking the lock," he muttered under his breath, which was immediately followed by a loud click and the door swinging open. Once he straightened out, Casey got a good glimpse of him and realized that the sunken-eyed, sagging man in front of her really was exhausted beyond belief.

Whether from delirious fatigue or overconfidence in his skills, he must have thought that it would be faster to pick the lock than to scrounge around in Charlie's pockets. That or...

Down on the floor, Charlie moaned once more. Yes, perhaps Ashton had feared waking him up by poking and prodding around. That would make sense.

Without warning, a most unwanted thought crossed Casey's mind. Had Ashton picked the lock that led into her brother's house? Had that been how he'd got the drop on him? She knew that it was irrelevant to the mission at hand, but the sister part of her wouldn't let the notion go.

"Let's get him in there," she said quickly, reaching down to pick Charlie up so that she had something, anything to do.

To her surprise, Ashton hurried over to heft Charlie's other shoulder. She'd been fully prepared to handle the thing on her own, but that too was her emotional and unprofessional side talking. Far better to have Ashton at least as much of a disadvantage as her.

It was an awkward thing, turning sideways to fit through the doorway. Ashton went first, then Charlie, who was even more dead to the world than he'd been before. Casey pulled up the rear, slipping the door closed in one fluid motion as she went.

The interior of the apartment was exactly as she remembered from the briefings she'd seen over the years, plus a few personal touches. It was sparsely decorated, which was Ulrich's mandate. Didn't want anything that could hide listening devices, mostly because he didn't trust his underlings to actually root them out with any measure of success. The living room that they immediately stepped into was populated exclusively by a gaudy couch and a massive television on the opposite wall. It was all Casey could do to avoid drawing comparisons to her own brother's bachelor pad from way back when.

Together, they eased Charlie down onto the couch, where he groaned pitifully and continued to exist as little more than a boneless heap. For a long moment, the pair just stared down at him.

"That's not good," Casey said.

"No, it is not," Ashton agreed. There was a glint of something in his eye, perhaps excitement. It wasn't enough to cut through the overall exhaustion that permeated his body, but it was something.

"Could die from a hit like that," Casey commented, injecting quite a bit more concern than she genuinely felt into her voice.

"Could indeed," Ashton said, utterly noncommittal. If she was exaggerating her concern, he was stifling his in equal measure.

This would have been a lot simpler if there was another couch or even just a single chair to sit down in, but there was absolutely nothing else decorating the sad little living room.

"So..." Ashton said slowly, thinking over his words. "Are you gonna leave now?"

"Are you gonna leave now?" Casey shot back, letting a bit of her true anger bleed through in what felt like a perfectly reasonable way. After all, it only made sense that this prostitute, deeply disturbed at the notion that she would lose out on a lucrative source of income, would rather wish to get a potential source of harm away from her client.

Ashton looked over at her, not quite sharply, but not nearly as sluggishly as his state would suggest. Was he faking his fatigue? "Lady, I'm going to have to ask him some very harsh questions. I don't think you wanna be here for that."

Or perhaps he was exactly as tired as he looked, so beyond his limits that he couldn't even think straight and come up with a compelling lie. Perhaps she could take advantage of that.

"I don't want him dead," she said slowly, her mouth only seconds behind her mind. "He's a nice guy."

Ashton raised an eyebrow at that.

"Alright, fine, he pays well," Casey corrected, folding her arms under her bust in a fashion that never failed to draw eyes, and today was no exception.

"Okay." With effort, Ashton looked up at her face, one eyebrow still quirked.

Now for the hard part.

"Look, I know how things are done around here. How about I go call an ambulance, and you have until they get here to get the answers you want. I don't want Charlie dead, you hear?"

Ashton stared at her, his eyes boring into her facade but finding nothing underneath. "How about you head out, wait five minutes, then give them a call?"

Casey feigned thoughtfulness, then shrugged and turned to leave. "Only five minutes," she called back over her shoulder as she made quite the show of leaving. In moments, the front door to the apartment was closed once more, leaving the men to resolve their disagreements.

Chapter 9

Waiting was always the hardest part. Training and hard numbers could only go so far. At a certain point, it just came down to gut instinct, how well you've read the opposition, and whether luck is on your side.

Casey waited beside the door, very much still inside the apartment, but only just. She'd wedged herself nicely into a corner of the entryway, where it was highly unlikely that Ashton would spot her unless he specifically came to the door to check if she'd actually left. She was gambling that he was in way too much of a rush to waste time on a thing like that, not when she could easily break her word and call for help the moment she was outside.

For her boldness, she was promptly rewarded. Footsteps moved away in such a hurry that she worried Ashton might be making a beeline for the fire escape. That fear dissipated as she listened to the clatter and clanging of pots and pans, followed by the sound of the kitchen faucet being turned on.

The running water ceased, and the footsteps returned, getting closer this time.

Sensing an opportunity, Casey crept closer. Still, in the shadowed entryway, she could see but a sliver of the living room, which was more than enough to confirm her suspicions. Ashton stood over Charlie, holding a decently sized saucepan full of water. Why he hadn't just brought a cup, Casey wasn't ready to guess.

One breath, then another. Ashton steadied himself, then poured the water down onto the unconscious Charlie.

Though he was in no position to appreciate it at the moment, Charlie should have been very thankful that he awoke at all. Brain injuries could be tricky like that. However, thankfulness for his continued survival was a distant, distant second to sheer outrage at his present state of affairs.

With a gasping cry, he flailed and surged upward from the couch, only to be immediately met by Ashton's sudden and forceful presence. With a shove, he pushed the disoriented and panicking man back down to the leather.

It was at that moment that Casey grasped the wisdom in bringing a pan instead of a cup, for the former made for a much more competent weapon. Hefting it in one hand, Ashton threatened his victim with a menacing sense of ease that left no doubt as to whether he was capable of murdering her brother in cold blood. If it weren't for her training, she would have shot him on the spot. The mission must come first.

"Hello, Charlie," Ashton said, his voice colder than she'd heard yet. "Been a while."

From her angle, it was difficult to see the exact expression on Charlie's face, but it was easy enough to see that he was frozen stiff in terror.

"What the hell are you doing out?" he asked, his voice a little more than a whimpering croak. "You were— you were supposed to be..."

Ashton's hand shook for a moment as though he would bring down his makeshift weapon upon the man's head and end it all in an instant. But then the shaking passed, and he took a breath to steady himself.

"Yeah, I'll bet this is something of a surprise to you. Don't worry though, this won't take long. I just need you to tell me exactly who set up the hit. That's all, just a name, then you can go."

Foolishly, Charlie sprang into action and tried to make his escape. Casey didn't belittle the man for making an effort but found much to criticize in his lack of planning. His attempt was sluggish, predictable, and foiled in an instant with another forceful shove from Ashton.

"I can't. He'll kill me!" Charlie cried, sounding like he was on the verge of actual tears. Casey only felt the slightest temptation to intervene and save his sorry hide.

Ashton replied, his voice low and dangerous but too indistinct for Casey to make out. Putting herself at even greater risk, she dared to step closer until she was exposed enough that either could notice her if they only turned to look.

"I told you, I don't KNOW!" Charlie shouted in reply. Not only could she hear them much better now, but she could see the wild whites of his eyes. The man was inches away from frothing at the lips, which just made her need to get names all the more imperative.

"Who killed Tommy, you stupid son of a bitch?" Ashton hissed, dropping the pan so that he could reach down and grab Charlie's collar with both hands. A sharp, violent shake nearly had the lower man's head shaking free from his spine.

No, she couldn't have heard that right. Casey was so tense she was nearly vibrating. It would be so easy to pull out her sidearm and kill one of them, kill both of them, and just get it over with. No, they didn't get to invoke Tommy here, not with their lying tongues. It was all a trick, she knew it in her bones.

The very moment that she made the decision not to intervene, Charlie jumped up for one last-ditch effort to escape. This time, he fared much better.

Ashton reeled back, surprised off balance for a single instant, but it was more than enough. Charlie struck wildly and without any thought, striking his captor in the side, in the chest, in the shoulder.

For his part, Ashton danced deftly backward, fending off the worst of it with a seasoned boxer's stance, protecting his vitals with his forearms and forcing Charlie into glancing blows.

Casey twitched, then pulled away, slipping further back into the hallway. No need to risk exposure if the fight took a turn, plus she could stop things from plenty far away. The benefits of carrying a gun, she mused as she took refuge deeper and deeper in her training.

Strangely, the explosion of tension had let the emotional turmoil drain out of the agent. Now, there was only careful observation as she watched the progress of the fight. When and if she stepped in, it would be dictated by honed reflex and years of drills rather than any emotional attachment.

Charlie and Ashton were of a size, but the former's brutal fear dictated the pace of the struggle. He swung and struck without precision, but if he was tiring himself out quickly, it was only bringing him onto even footing with a man that looked not to have enjoyed a good night's rest in weeks, if not months.

Or years, Casey contemplated darkly. She could only hope that he'd been deprived of all life's simplest pleasures in his years in prison. Hell, maybe there would be some cosmic justice in the world after all, and maybe he would be killed by some brute thug in his apartment. Wouldn't that be something?

For a moment, the idea felt more and more compelling. She could even step in and kill him, presenting herself to Charlie as his savior and gleaning information from him in the aftermath.

But no, that plan was foolhardy at best. Charlie was completely out of it, and it was entirely likely that he would turn on her the very moment that Ashton was out of the picture. If that happened, then she would be deprived of the information that both of them had.

As she watched, she saw Charlie make the first intelligent move he'd made all evening. Amidst his unrelenting assault, he suddenly leapt back and reached for the couch, burying his hand between the cushions. A stashed weapon?

A part of her had to commend Ashton for his presence of mind. It must have been overwhelmingly tempting to take the momentary separation to recover, but he saw the danger as clear as day. Leaping forward, he landed a clean blow to Charlie's jaw right as glinting steel pulled out of the space between cushions. Before Charlie could even get a grip on the knife, he was falling down to the floor.

"Who got Tommy killed?" Ashton demanded, his voice beyond hoarse as he gasped for breath. "Tell me, you little dipshit. I'm sick and fucking tired of taking the blame for something I didn't do, so you're going to answer me, and—"

"Stop, please," Charlie whimpered, but something in his tone caught Casey's attention. She eased towards the doorway, step by silent step.

"Answer the question," Ashton growled. He was nearly gasping, and Casey could tell that it was a struggle just for him to remain upright.

"Come on, man," Charlie whimpered once again, his hands moving slowly behind his back. He'd lost the knife at some point, and from Ashton's vantage point, he likely couldn't even see the motion. Even if he could, by the way, he was rocking back and forth, he may have been too tired to even notice.

"Name," Ashton grunted. His fingers tensed into a fist, then loosened. Was he even capable of finishing the fight?

"Ulrich ordered it, man, you know that," Charlie pleaded, his fingers inches away from the hilt. His eyes darted back, and if he'd been a little more aware, he surely would have spotted the woman watching with absolute focus. But he was not aware of his surroundings, instead so completely focused on his treachery that he didn't even pay attention to the tower of rage standing over him.

"I knew it," Ashton said, almost seeming to relax. "All this time—"

Charlie seized his moment, snarling as he leapt upward, swinging the knife wildly and hoping that it would cut true. He was fast, Casey could admit that, but he wasn't even close to fast enough for it to matter.

Three things happened in quick succession. A crack rang out, then Ashton turned at the sound and narrowly avoided getting his throat slit, then Charlie slammed into the floor, a slave of his own momentum.

When the dust settled, Casey had her gun trained firmly on her unmoving target, and Ashton was staring at her in blinking confusion. For an instant, it looked like he was about to say something, and then he fell.

Chapter 10

Awareness came slowly. Ashton knew who he was, and he knew his crimes, but everything recent was a blur. There was pain, there was betrayal, there was prison, and then...

Slowly, he sat up, his muscles protesting all the while. He was in a bed, but it was none he had ever seen or felt before. No lights were on, but through the window, he could see the distant glow of a full moon.

Every movement burned, but as he lifted a hand to his face, he grazed the unmistakable feel of bandaging on his shoulder. That was all it took to remember the fight and Charlie. The last bit though, that felt more like a hallucination than anything else. Surely that prostitute hadn't stuck around, pulled a gun, and shot Charlie dead. The knife swipe aimed at his throat though that had been real enough. As had his narrow dodge.

Of course, that just raised the question of how the hell he'd ended up in this bed. Someone had certainly put him here, apparently after bandaging up his injuries. By now, he was quite certain that he'd been far too exhausted to manage anything of the kind on his own.

With a grunt and a groan, he worked himself to the edge of the bed and rose to his feet. Whatever discomfort he may suffer paled in comparison to the truth that was so tantalizingly close. It had been Ulrich.

He could see it in his mind, just as clearly as if it was yesterday. Tommy, perforated in his own room, filled with holes in the comfort of his home, and left to be discovered by Ashton. They'd known he would stumble upon the body, and they set it up so he would take the fall. All his years of wondering if he'd gone insane and actually murdered his best friend, all of those sleepless nights wasted in feverish fear of his own sanity.

Now that he was near enough to taste victory, he could not falter. Oh, he could die, that would be a fine enough outcome, so long as he took that treacherous bastard with him.

Thus committed to a course, he felt his way through the dark, stumbling his way over to the door. However, he didn't even get a chance to cross the threshold before she emerged out of the darkness, a gaunt spectre that shone as pale and terrible and beautiful as the moon.

His voice caught in his throat, denying any surprised yelp. Ashton stumbled backwards, barely able to keep his footing.

"You shouldn't be up," she said quietly, stepping into the room. She looked nothing like the escort from earlier, yet he knew that it must be her. The way her eyes pierced him left no doubt in his heart.

In an instant, he calculated that his chances of successful resistance were, at their most optimistic, not good. He was injured, he hadn't slept a full night, and she was still armed, as far as he knew.

"I suppose I have you to thank for tending to my injuries," he said as he took a step back to match her step forward. He tried to stand upright and relaxed, but it pained him dearly.

"That's right." She extended her hand, taking a step forward, but he had no more room to retreat. His back bumped up against the wall, and he could only bear witness as her fingers caressed his cheek.

He averted his gaze, but that just forced him to look down at the white silk night robe that she was wearing. It was an astonishing work of elegance, clinging to her and fluttering in the moonlight like nothing he'd ever seen. She could not have planned it better, to be squarely in the light cast by the window.

Slowly, her fingers explored, half in a clinical search for injuries, half with a more tender and terrifying curiosity. She brushed past his stubble, down his neck, and over the densest bandaging. He could still feel the sting of the blade where her hand passed.

"Good, it looks like you haven't opened your wound up. However, I don't think you got nearly as much sleep as you need." Her eyes rose, demanding that he meet them. There was something that stirred a deep memory within him, but before he could latch onto it, she was moving once more, gently pulling his arm towards the bed.

Ashton obeyed, barely able to stay upright. His physical ailments were bad, but his fear of his own desire was even worse. How many years had it been since he'd actually been alone with a woman?

"Why did you come back earlier? I thought you left to call for help," he said as he slumped down onto the edge of the bed. She joined him, maintaining enough distance that they weren't touching, but not so much that he could ignore her.

Her shrug was noncommittal, marked mainly by the bed creaking under them. "Had a hunch. Wasn't actually going to call an ambulance anyway. Don't want their attention around here, and I'm not the only one."

Ashton nodded at that. He could accept such an explanation, especially with the kind of people who walked these streets, and yet...

Her hand set atop his, and all other thoughts were annihilated.

"Where are we?" he whispered, more concerned with distracting himself from doing something stupid than really looking for an answer.

"We haven't gone anywhere," she replied, her voice just as quiet, and a thousand times more seductive.

His mind reeled with the implications. They were in an apartment with a dead body? Or had she moved the body, and if so, who had helped her? Wasn't someone going to come and find them, and very soon?

But once more, she forced his thoughts from his head, rising to stand before him. He had no choice but to look up, to behold the woman who looked more ghost than human.

"You..." she trailed off, leaving him craving the rest of her thought, if only to hear her voice once more.

"I?"

"You must sleep," she said simply.

He knew she was right, and the next thing he knew, he was falling into endless softness.

Chapter 11

He'd been up almost an hour. Granted, most of that had been spent lying in bed, staring up at the ceiling as the sun rose outside, but he had eventually risen completely. However, he had then stumbled over to a chair that she'd strategically placed in the corner of the bedroom and promptly slumped down into it, unseeing as he struggled with his inner demons, whose existence Casey did not doubt one bit.

Last night had gone very effectively. A little teasing, a little evaluating of his mental state, a little imposing of her will upon him, and then he'd gone straight to sleep. Now, she just had to take the next step. An incredibly easy and familiar step if it wasn't for her personal involvement and emotional tumult.

She'd gone out during the night and retrieved one of her supply caches, which she'd done while agents on her team were quietly disposing of Charlie's body. Once she'd gotten back to the apartment, she'd feared that Ashton might have woken or escaped, but he had still been slumbering heavily.

Casey looked herself over once more, trying very hard to keep her memories in the past, where they belonged. There was no need to dredge up painful recollections of how she'd wanted to impress her brother's friends and shown off far more skin than a teenager should dare. That her wish should manifest in this terrible, terrible way was nearly enough to curl her lip.

Her long-sleeved shirt was as tight as it was soft, perfectly accentuating the swell of her chest and inviting a touch in every way possible. Her skirt promised easy access that she was fully prepared to follow up on, and her dark stockings contrasted nicely with the pale image she'd presented to him last night.

She strolled into the bedroom but was surprised when he didn't look in her direction immediately. Ashton simply kept staring sightlessly at the wall, focused entirely on his own thoughts. Well, she could work with that easily enough.

Casey sauntered over until she was standing right in front of him. Slowly, he came back to his senses, only to laboriously crawl his gaze upwards, covering every inch of her body before he met her eyes. It wasn't a languid, lusty route that he took, but the haggard lethargy of a man beset on all sides. However, that only made it all the more satisfying to see his breathing quicken as he took stock of the body on display for him. Such was her power that she could inspire carnal obsession in even the most preoccupied of men.

But she didn't allow him a moment to breathe. She stepped behind the chair, resting her hands on his shoulders, and let him sweat for a long, long moment.

"How are your injuries?" she asked, her voice little more than a purr.

"Not... so bad," he said, tensing beneath her touch.

"Hm."

Her fingers kneaded, working into his flesh, forcing him to choose between maintaining his tension and melting into putty in her hands.

"Do you do this often?" he asked, the harshness of his question at odds with the volume of his whisper. She didn't begrudge him for this last pitiful act of resistance. It was certainly common enough in men that were about to fall prey to her charms and saw the end approaching but could do nothing to avert it.

"Do I do what often, Ashton?" she asked right back, her voice as sweet as can be. To heighten the effect, she leaned down to create the sensation of her mouth drawing closer to his ear. Not all the way, not yet. There would be time enough for that yet.

"Massage men, that murder your clients?" He did a good enough job until the last word when an uncontrollable shiver ran down his body. He could try to hide it all he wanted, but she could feel everything.

"You might be surprised," she said, bending down even lower. He could surely feel her breath on his ear if she was so inclined, and she very much was. "If all your clients are dangerous men, then it will inevitably happen that you service one who has killed another."

He snorted at that, sagging into the chair just a fraction. Bit by bit, she knew she was dismantling his defenses. There were a million things he could say to that, a million different ways he could argue, but the fact that he could muster exactly none of them told the entire story.

Casey moved her fingers, pausing in the light massage for just a moment. She felt the bandage, searching for wetness and any reaction from him. He stiffened but didn't wince or moan in agony. The cut wasn't dangerously deep, but there was some danger of him opening it up again.

"Why are you doing this?" he whispered, an entirely new hoarseness present in his voice. This, she knew from experience, was fear.

The moment of truth, then. Time to see if she could wrap this bastard around her finger. All her questions could wait until later. For now, there was just her training against his willpower.

Casey bent low, her lips brushing up against his ear, her hands lightly resting on his shoulders, rubbing gently. "You look like a man who's been deprived for a long time. Let's just say I have a soft spot."

It shouldn't have worked. It wouldn't have worked, but she knew just how lonely this man was. If he really was Ashton, if he really had just escaped from prison, then it had been more than a decade since he'd known the touch of anyone affectionate. She'd kept up on his affairs in prison, and every source indicated that he was a loner at best and actively ostracized at worst. All it took was a little offer of companionship, no matter how fleeting, no matter how suspicious, and he would collapse.

And she was right.

He sagged back into the chair, releasing all his woes with a gusty sigh. Casey leaned forward, reaching down, letting her hands glide down his sides, caressing his skin through his shirt. Her chest pressed up against the back of his head, cushioning him, providing the pillow that he'd so long been denied.

Casey was a professional, but she also recognized that the best operatives lent more truth to the dance than lies. As such, she had no problem letting herself admire his physique and the exact nature of the man hiding beneath the grit, grime, and suffering.

Last night, he'd been exhausted to the point of looking like a demon. Once she'd cleaned his wounds and washed off the worst of his filth, she'd found a body kept in excellent condition. Muscled, but for purpose instead of vanity. Sharp cheeks made sharper by hunger, haunted eyes that called out for a woman to save him, and lips that simply demanded a kiss, if only to say that you were the only one to appreciate them in recent memory. He hit every perverse affection that she held, appealing to her on a primal level that she didn't care to examine.

Her fingers dipped beneath the edge of his jeans, caressing his skin and reveling in how his entire body stiffened at the sensitivity. She went no further, satisfying herself with brushing her fingertips along his waistband.

"When was the last time you felt the touch of a woman?" she murmured, finding herself legitimately curious about his answer.

"Too long," he croaked. His hands gripped the arms of the chair, white with effort as he restrained himself.

"You don't have to hold back, you know," she whispered, letting her fingers slide down even deeper until they pressed into a tangled forest of curly hair. "I like it when men know what they want. I like it, even more, when they take it."

That didn't break him, but it sure came close. The dom in him urged him to take control but this had to be her choice. As a former cop he never condoned prositution but if she ws offering freely and after all this time. He sure as hell wan't going to turn her down.

"How can you enjoy this? Isn't it just your job?" he asked without a shred of guile. Poor man, he probably didn't even know what he was saying, only that he had to say something to distract himself from the incomprehensible temptation rubbing up against him.

"I think you might be under some misapprehensions." Casey couldn't help but giggle when he shuddered beneath her. "Professionals can still enjoy their work."

"Is that so?" he asked breathlessly.

"That is definitely so."

She waited, as much for her own delight as his, and lazily watched his crotch. What was just a crease in his jeans, and what was the outline of his cock? How big was he?

Her fingers advanced cautiously, which necessitated leaning down even lower, pressing her breasts against his neck even harder. She could feel the slickness between their skin, his sweat mixing with hers.

She searched, brushing against his thick hair and questing for his manhood.

"Will I be impressed by your cock?" she murmured.

He answered that with his tongue but without words. Turning his face, he fell into a deep, passionate kiss of her neck. Sucking, draining her dry, he hungrily, possessively sought to leave a mark. Casey couldn't say she was displeased with his ardor.

One hand still teasing at his crotched, her other slipped up beneath his shirt, caressing his abs and outlining what muscles she may find. Last night, she'd seen and felt everything during her tender ministrations, but context changed everything. What she'd merely cataloged and treated before now served to ignite a fire in her belly and below.

He pulled down on her, surprising a gasp from her lips. At the same moment, the motion pushed her fingers past his cock, sliding over it. She reflexively gripped it, marveling at how perfectly it seemed to fit in her hand. Oh yes, she was quite impressed.

Chapter 12

Ashton was at the edge. He thought he could stay in control, but the damn woman just kept pulling and pushing. Fine, if that's the game she wanted to play, then he could show her how sorely she'd underestimated him.

At least, that's what he'd thought right up until the point when she grabbed his cock. From there, all bets were off.

His devouring kiss of her neck took on a new edge as he reached up to grab her hair, twisting it around his hand and pull her lips to his. He was only as forceful as he needed to be and painstakingly gentle in all other respects. He feared himself, and he feared her, but more than that, he feared breaking either one of them.

Her eyes were wide and shocked when he dove into the kiss. After that, she could keep staring all she wanted, but his eyes were firmly shut. His hips rose and bucked gently, forcing some motion into her hand.

She was far less tender than he. He waited to see what she did, thinking to match her exploration with his tongue, but she forced herself in, demanding that he receive her. It was hardly how expected things to go, but nothing he could complain about.

Holding his eyes with her, she unfastened his jeans and lowered the zipper. His cock sprang out as if escaping a prison, incredibly long and thick, the veins engorged and bulging. With the same slow, deliberate movements, she sheathed him in a condom. He'd never met someone he'd given anyone to who he had given so much control over him.

One set of fingers, then another, groping him, sliding up and down, gently squeezing and releasing. The pad of her thumb slid over the top with the lightest of pressure, then one hand settled on a grip, and the slow, painstaking pumping began.

She pulled away from the kiss, sucking in a deep breath as they both opened their eyes. There was an intensity in her gaze that had certainly been there before but was taking on entirely new meanings. He'd known she was a prostitute from the start, of course, but to see it in action...

"How did you know Charlie?" she asked, and as if anticipating that his first reaction would be confusion, she pumped faster and faster, biting her lip as she concentrated on milking him.

"We... used to be friends. Coworkers," he managed, barely fighting off the urge to groan.

She groaned, but it was flavored with a thick and desirous moan. She reached down and took his hand, then pulled it up to press upon her breast. Even though her shirt looked thick, he could feel everything beneath, and it felt so perfect.

He squeezed, testing her reactions slowly. With each caress of her breast, she answered with a languid twist of her wrist, driving his cock closer and closer to final release.

"And what happened to sour relations?"

He wasn't going to answer that. He had no intention whatsoever of revealing his secrets, right up until she pulled away, moved to the side of the chair, and leaned over until her ass was sticking out, her mouth hovering an inch above his cock. Then, she plunged down.

"He stabbed me in the back," Ashton panted, though it did nothing to distract from the sensation. Her mouth was so very generous, so willing to take all that he had to give. She toyed with the head, teasing and licking, swirling her tongue in circles, exhibiting a level of mastery that he had never even dreamed possible.

Driven purely by nature, he reached over to grab her ass, which was positioned at the most convenient angle possible. It was so easy to grip a cheek, to lightly slap, to slide a hand down, and...

She pulled away just long enough to throw a smirk back his way. "Are you planning to stab me in the back?"

He opened his mouth, then shut it promptly as the full meaning descended onto him. Instead, he just leaned his head back on the back of the chair and let the tactile beauty of the moment fill him. The escort bobbed up and down, taking him deeper and deeper into her mouth. His fingers searched down, so very thankful for her skirt and the panties that were so easy to part. His fingers slipped in, and he was immediately rewarded by a choking gasp of pleasure that did wondrous things to his cock, trapped as it was between her lips.

"So, did you decide if you're impressed with my cock?"

She answered with exquisite torture that made his knees shake in spite of the fact that he was sitting down. All the way, lower and lower, further and further, she took him in her mouth. Deepthroating, a pleasure that he'd never experienced before, was almost too much for him. He nearly came on the spot and was saved from doing so not by his own discipline but by his lover's cruel designs.

She pulled away, rising back to her full height, but doing nothing about the fingers that were slowly slipping in and out of her. Rather, she sidled up to him, carefully pulling herself up onto the chair until she was straddling him. Thankfully, she wasn't stimulating his manhood anymore, choosing to put her weight more on his belly than anything else. Her hands lazily wrapped around the back of his neck, cradling him, inviting him to look up at her.

Or, as he reached down to lift up her shirt and pull it up until her breasts were fully bared, providing the perfect height for him to admire her chest. He'd never before considered the merits of a nice, thick shirt rolled up to just above the breasts, perfectly exposing her in a way that was so sinfully easy to disguise if one were caught. It brought him back to a teenage excitement that he'd long since considered beaten out of him, and his cock was every bit as ambitious as it had been back in those golden days.

"May I kiss them?" he asked with mock seriousness, looking up to her with a pleading look on his face.

Oddly, that made her grin. Perhaps they were more kindred than he'd thought.

"I suppose you have my permission, so long as you don't damage anything. You break them, you buy them."

"Damage them? I only asked for a kiss."

"Perhaps you need a lesson in how destructive kisses can be then."

With that, she leaned forward, burying his face in her chest, denying him a chance to breathe and forcing him to bask in the glory of her closeness. Her scent, her sweat, her skin, the fullness of her breasts, and the temptation of her nipples, it was the entirety of his world for a moment that seemed to stretch out to infinity. He licked and kissed and reached behind her to hold her close, delighting in how each of his different explorations was received. She twisted and groaned appreciatively at each lick, but it was the hug that brought the breathiest and most precious sigh of contentment.

Perhaps it was his years of torment, perhaps it was an overactive sense of chivalry, but he did find something compelling in the sense of closeness that even carnal ecstasy could not match. The idea that she might feel safe in his embrace might even wish to cuddle up next to him, appealing to him in a way that spilling his seed could not compete with.

But, blessed was Ashton, for there was no competition required. As he was in the process of discovering, he didn't need to have one or the other. He could have a mouthful of luscious breast, and a hug one moment, then she could be shifting her weight backward the next.

She set his cock against her opening, sliding it up and down and getting it wet, she realized—only one second before he drove inside her in a ruthless thrust that wrung a cry from her. Her insides convulsed around the thick erection in wavering jolts of pleasure.

"Fuck, you feel incredible," he growled, "and I am going to take you hard." He lowered his voice. "Because I want to. Because I can."

Somehow her bones trickled right out of her body. He gave a deep laugh. With an implacable grip on her hips, he drove up into her, hard as he'd promised, hammering into her until the driving rhythm somehow caught her like a hooked fish, yanking her arousal up from the depths. And then she was lost as each plunging thrust pushed her closer and closer.

As her need increased, she tried to push her hips back to meet his thrusts. He slapped her butt, and as her insides clenched like a fist at the shocking sting, he said, "If you want more, I will give you more—at my discretion."

How could he talk now? She shoved back toward his cock again. A second later, she realized his meaning as he pushed her legs so far apart that she couldn't do anything. And then he curved his hands on her thighs and yanked her against his groin, sheathing his cock to the hilt each time.

He controlled her completely yet gave her exactly what she wanted, and the knowledge thrilled through her and exploded her into a climax as quickly as if he'd set off a bomb inside her. Her head spun. Despite her orgasm, each implacable thrust sent her even higher until her body shook with brutal pleasure. His hands tightened, lifting her right off his cock. He growled and pressed inside so deeply she felt his cock hit her womb and then the jerking sensations as he climaxed.

He breathed, the first in a long while. Long, heaving, shuddering breaths filled him with air, and he released her. If he'd expected her to pull away, he was sorely mistaken. As he leaned back into the chair, she fell forward with him, very nearly curling up on his shoulder as her fingers twisted in the fabric upon his shoulders. She rose and fell with such deep breaths that he couldn't help but wonder what that might look like from a more advantageous position. With how impressive her breasts were, he knew that it must be quite the sight.

"That was rather nice," she murmured up against him, so close that he could feel the vibrations more than he could hear the words. Half of him was tempted to feign misunderstanding just so he could experience that again.

"Impressive even, I dare say," he said, shifting slightly in the chair to make her more comfortable. She didn't laugh, but she did rumble in a way that suggested a combination of groaning and purring.

Without meaning to, he began to stroke her hair, delighting in the way the strands separated in his fingers. If he held it up to the light, it shone with the early morning sunlight streaming in through the window.

Inevitably, his thoughts drifted back to the more dire circumstances ahead of him. Wonderful though this had been, perhaps that's all it signified. Perhaps this was the last bit of happiness he would have in this life. It was fitting, in a way, he supposed. After the suffering came vindication, a tiny glimpse of pleasure that could not even begin to compensate for all his lost years, and then the finality of an impossible task achieved.

It was, he decided, not a terrible way to go out. And with that thought, he slipped away into a drowsing nap the likes of which he had not known for more than a decade.

Chapter 13

Ashton opened his eyes, unsettled on a fundamental level. Something was wrong, but he couldn't quite put a finger on it, and the sense of unease only grew as he took in his surroundings. The bed beneath him was soft but not so soft that it was uncomfortable. The light streaming in through the window was the pleasant gold of late afternoon. Most damningly, he didn't have a sick feeling in his gut nor a ghastly pounding behind his eyes. It was, by every measure he could take, nothing more than a dream.

That's when he realized what was wrong. He'd never had a dream like this before. He'd spent so many years in the grip of haunting nightmares that he couldn't even remember the last time that he'd had a simple, uncomplicated dream.

He rolled over without thinking much of it, only to find himself staring at the fluttering eyelashes of the most beautiful woman he'd ever seen. Her graceful elegance teetered on the edge of wakefulness as if the smallest puff of air might rouse her. Something about her struck him as familiar, but it was an ephemeral, fleeting feeling. It was, he decided after a moment's consideration, just his mind playing tricks on him. All of this was a product of his mind playing tricks on him. There was no sense in dispelling the comforting warmth any sooner than was absolutely necessary.

"Good morning," he whispered, strangely pleased at how the words felt on his tongue. How many years had it been since he'd had occasion to whisper sweet nothings to a lover?

One eye cracked open, leveling a sleepy stare with an edge of steel that left him feeling rather disconcerted. It certainly didn't look like the gaze of someone who had just woken up.

"Good morning," she replied, her voice so sultry and tantalizing that his heart skipped a beat. The gentle movement of her lips and the soft whiteness of her teeth hadn't come from his memory but from every fantasy he'd ever had. A dream indeed.

"Sleep well?" he asked, eager to draw this languid pleasure out for as long as possible. Primal coupling wasn't even on his mind, but he thought a simple hug would not be unpleasant. Barring that, some light, the meaningless conversation would do well enough. "You certainly look it."

Something tiny and barely noticeable flickered across her face. A twitch of the lip here, a narrowing of the eye there, then it was gone. If Ashton hadn't been quite so intent on studying the face and committing it to his nostalgic memory, he likely wouldn't have noticed it at all.

And then she was smiling, the lazy and confident grin of a sated predator. She stretched, still facing him, which had the rather enticing effect of jutting her bust a few inches towards him.

"Yes, it was a wonderful rest," she purred, never taking her eyes off him for a single moment. She was watching to see what he did as if perpetually calculating the right thing to say and do next. "And how was yours, Ashton?"

Worries crept at the edge of his consciousness. There were plenty of things to fret about, but he refused to consider any of them. All that could wait until he woke up. For now, just let him enjoy this one tiny fragment of peace.

"It was..." he trailed off, looking down to see her hand slowly crossing the distance between them. It was not a cautious gesture but a study in sensuality, drawing the eye to exactly how those long fingers moved and what they might accomplish. That they settled on his hip was hardly a reassurance that her motives were pure. If anything, it just meant that there would be plenty of agonizingly slow progress as she crept inward.

His heart raced, but not nearly as much as his mind. He didn't want to think, he just wanted everything to be calm. His hand settled atop hers, thwarting any untoward ambitions she might have had. Her eyes met his, a decidedly seductive question lurking beneath those luscious eyelashes.

"Maybe later. Can we just enjoy this for now?"

She pulled her hand back so quickly that he didn't even have a chance to protest. While he didn't want that, he was not at all opposed to feeling the closeness of another human being. But her eyes didn't suggest the sort of hurt petulance that he'd expected. Instead, there was only cold speculation.

"Are you under the impression that this is a dream?"

He stared at her for a time, then rolled onto his back. He could still see her out of the corner of his eye, and she had propped herself up on an elbow to look down on him.

"It has to be a dream," Ashton said at last. "There's no other explanation."

At that, she closed the distance once more, stretching her leg out and laying it across his. It was a possessive touching of the thighs, and her toes tickled at his calf.

"No other explanation? Really?" Her voice dripped with a combination of bitter sarcasm and amusement.

He thought on that for a moment. Memories, fantasies, nightmares, and regrets could be indistinguishable at times. Maybe it wasn't that way for other people, but it certainly was for him. There was only one constant in his life: getting justice for Tommy. Beyond that, everything was negotiable.

It was theoretically possible that the bits and pieces he remembered from last night were true. It was technically plausible that he'd made love to a woman shortly after the pair of them had effectively ended a man's life.

"I find it hard to believe that what I remember is what happened," he said after a while. He kept his eyes fixed to the ceiling, suddenly wondering if this was the sight a dead man had woken up to each morning and would never wake up to again, thanks in part to him. He nearly laughed mirthlessly at the realization that this was becoming something of a trend for the ceiling, seeing as Ashton would be dead soon enough as well.

Her leg shifted upon him, teasing upwards but not quite touching his excited flesh. A hand drifted across his chest, her fingers trailing across his flesh and raising hairs in their wake.

"Does this feel real?"

He thought about that, but mostly, he just enjoyed basking in the luxury of her whisper.

"It does feel real," he agreed, closing his eyes. If this was going to be how he died, then so be it. He was exhausted.

"You have rather wicked nightmares," she mused. It wasn't a question but a statement of fact.

"Hope I didn't thrash around while I slept." He tried to keep his tone light but had no idea if he succeeded. The pain was still raw, and after so many years, he was pretty sure that would never stop being the case. Not until he was dead and buried, justice or no.

"No, but you did mutter a few words."

Ashton would have tensed at that eight or nine years ago. By now, he'd spoken whatever he would speak in his sleep, and to enough ears, on the cellblock, that word would have surely gotten back to anyone in Ulrich's camp that cared.

For a moment, he considered outright asking this beautiful goddess if he was truly awake. He shook that idea off quickly. No need to shatter the illusion any faster than was strictly necessary.

"I've had nightmares for quite a few years," he said slowly, feeling his way as he went. "I've done things I regret and likewise regretted things I didn't do."

"Such as?"

Her prodding set him at ease, if only slightly. If this was just an artifact of his subconscious, then what harm was there in unburdening himself to his psyche once more? He'd done it plenty of times in the past, so why not one last time for good measure?

The words came slowly at first, but soon they were tumbling forth without end. His hands, so neatly folded when he began to describe the circumstances of misspent youth, were soon clutching the sheets at his side with white knuckles.

There was nothing particularly noteworthy about the story. He'd hung out with the wrong crowd and started down the slippery slope of belonging and familiarity with the wrong sort of people. Soon enough, he was looking up to men that were as charismatic as they were soulless. The deeper he got, the more they asked of him, until he was deep enough in petty crimes that there was a threat of evidence always hanging over his head. Oh, sure, they never specifically said they would turn him in and tell the cops about all his little adventures, but they certainly hinted at it.

But that was really only half of his life at that point. The other half, the better half, was the childhood friendship he'd always had with Tommy Anderson. Inseparable growing up, they started to drift apart around the time when Ashton began to hang out with Ulrich's boys. It was also the time the police recruited him to work undercover in Ulrich's organization. They still saw each other from time to time, but it had led to arguments and angry partings more often than not. If only he'd listened to Tommy back then to get out before he got himself killed. If only he'd listened to his conscience.

He'd said nothing of consequence so far, yet it all burdened him so heavily and speaking the words aloud healed his soul in a way that nothing else had ever managed. He turned to look at the woman lying by his side, expecting to see boredom or polite interest, but instead, he found an absolutely unreadable specter. Her eyes bored into him, demanding that he continue the story, but whatever she felt beyond that was guarded deep.

And so he continued. The crux of the matter was as simple as it was difficult to speak aloud, yet he somehow managed. In his ambition to advance in Ulrich's organization, he'd been given a simple test of loyalty. All he had to do was steal something from his best friend. Not because the organization actually cared about what was stolen, but because they wanted him to commit an act of betrayal that would tie him to the membership forever. Prove you have what it takes, nothing to it.

The mistake had seemed so inconsequential at the time. All he did was say no. He didn't even continue to deny them, he just said it once, then thought about it, then changed his mind. Apparently, refusing them a single time was all it took because once he finally agreed to carry out their task, it had already been too late.

The next day, he built up the courage to break into Tommy's place to keep his cover. The fact that he already had a key, entrusted to him by his best friend even though their harsh disagreements hurt far more than it helped.

When he'd stepped across that threshold, he'd been so focused on his own terror that he hadn't even noticed the off smell. If he had, maybe he would have been a little more prepared when he peeked into the bedroom and found a tortured, bullet-riddled body that had just enough of a face remaining to make its identity clear. He couldn't save him. He tried. He tried so hard to save him, but there was too much blood. He begged Tommy to stay with him as he watched his best friend take his last breath. Maybe he would have turned and run fast enough to avoid the oncoming sirens, to keep his cover. But why when he was the reason Tommy was dead in the first place. New York PD had claimed they had no connection to him, so he'd been hung out to dry and when the local headlines read local man killed by Ashton Malick. A jury had came to that verdict too.

He didn't realize he'd run out of steam and slipped into a miserable silence until the woman at his side moved. He tensed, dreading the comforting touch that would surely come, only to belatedly realize that she had turned to face away from him. Her shoulders rose and fell in what could be nothing but great emotional turmoil.

"I..."

Abruptly, Ashton realized that he had absolutely no idea what to say. He'd expected some sort of practiced tenderness.

After all, if this was a dream, then that would make sense. If it was a nightmare, then he expected some brutal recrimination and mockery. And, if he actually was awake by some miracle, then this was a prostitute, so she'd probably had her fair share of men breaking down in front of her. A professional "There, there" seemed proper protocol in such a scenario, but this was far beyond the limits of his imagination.

"Are you alright?" he asked, reaching out to settle a hand on her shoulder, then thought better of it. Changing his approach, he rose up to a sitting position.

Seconds passed, and the wracking heaves of her body ceased. There was no sound, and it was enough to make Ashton wonder if he'd gone deaf. It was such a controlled and intimate outburst, so very closed off from the world. Even witnessing it felt like he was intruding on someone's most private sanctum. He had already asked her once, and decided that it would not do to press. Instead, he would merely wait.

Chapter 14

There was never a single moment where she let her guard down. That's what Casey kept telling herself. It was true, in a certain sense, since she never kept her hand far from the weapon that was hidden at the small of her back. Even when her other hand was teasing and tempting the flesh of her victim, it would only take an instant to bring the knife up for a killing blow.

And yet, she could not ignore the aching turmoil that accompanied Ashton's words. The resurfaced memories of her brother would have been enough, but to confront the possibility that she'd spent a huge portion of her life hating the wrong man was almost too much to bear. Oh, she was still ready to end his life in a flash, but that was more honed reflexes than anything else. If she was on the verge of death, her body would still remember how to dispatch a target that grew too unruly in bed. The mission always came first.

It was in this single-minded devotion to duty that she found refuge. Turning back to face the man who was now sitting and watching her with a pensive look, she had to try harder than ever before to keep her features a composed mask.

This would be much easier if she didn't have to look at his face, so she moved with lazy sensuality until she was behind him. Her hands settled gently on his shoulders, and she stared hard at the nape of his neck. He'd stopped breathing and felt about ready to bolt, but the instant that her fingers began to squeeze and knead, he very nearly melted.

"Sorry if that was too heavy," he murmured, sinking into a boneless slouch, yet not putting all his weight back against her. Perhaps he was too much of a gentleman for that, Casey thought with a humorless grin.

"Not the worst I've heard," she said half-truthfully. If he wanted to believe her to be nothing more than an escort that had the stomach for listening to confessions, then who was she to stop him?

"Honestly," he began with a surprising edge to his voice, "the only thing I care about now is making sure that the bastards are brought to justice. I don't care if I have to go back to prison for it, not so long as they pay."

Massages were a rather convenient way to convert sudden bursts of tension into a bit of deep tissue rubbing. Ashton shuddered in her hands, almost in a macabre mirror of an orgasm, but then he was relaxing even more than before. He didn't notice for even a moment how she froze and shuddered at his words.

"So, are you going to report them to the police or something?" Casey asked. Her hands drifted down to work on his back, using her thumbs to get deep near his spine.

"No" His voice could not have been more bitter if he'd tried. "I was the police and that got me no where. So, I went to prison. I alone."

She waited for him to continue. The only sound in the room was his heavy breathing that verged on groaning, but that was all he had to say on the subject.

"That's an amusing lack of respect for the law, especially from a former undercover cop" she commented.

His terse laugh reverberated through her fingers. "Sorry, that's just funny coming from someone in your... line of work."

"I suppose it is, isn't it?" Her fingers traced delicate lines down his back, which once again brought him to tense anticipation. Where would she strike next? She considered reaching down and taking a firm hold of things... but perhaps not yet.

"Do you work for Ulrich?" he asked suddenly, but his tone was more resigned than accusing.

Casey continued her massage, thinking long and hard about her answer. She felt a kindred yearning, to tell the truth, to share in the man's grief, but was there something to be gained by deceiving the man? Was there some speck of truth that could be gleaned from further lies?

Probably not, she told herself as her fingers slowed to a crawl. She was clinging onto the familiar, and she knew it. Everything was so easy and clear when she knew who to hate but to accept the fact that she had been wrong...

One misstep and the dam would break. Professionalism kept her sardonic and putting one step in front of the other, but could she bear to let go of that? Could she be vulnerable for just one moment? Didn't he deserve the truth from her, in penance for hate that he'd never even known she bore him?

"No," she decided in the end. "I do not work for Ulrich. Never have, never will."

He relaxed at that, which she couldn't help but feel was a foolish move on his part. "Why are you so quick to trust me at my word?"

"Because I'm tired," he said and then was silent.

Casey kneaded the muscles of the man that had played a role in the slaying of her brother, albeit a much smaller and more blameless role than she'd imagined before. Still, she could sympathize with simply being tired of it all. Maybe nobody else would understand, but the two of them certainly did.

"I could kill you," she said, and neither of them believed it to be a lie.

"I know," he said, not even bothering to hide the heaviness of it all. "But if I'm going to die, I might as well do it clinging to the one shred of comfort I've felt in the last ten years. Whether you work for Ulrich or not, whether this is a trap or not, it's all just too much."

"Too much," she repeated in a murmur. Gingerly, she slipped her arms past and around him, holding the man in a twisted, loose hug. It would have been easy for her to do even if he'd been the most despicable filth on the planet and had put the bullets in her brother. After all, it's what she was trained to do. Offering comfort that veiled her threats and manipulations were as easy as breathing, but now that it came to sharing intimacy with the only person that she'd resonated with, not just in the last few years, but in her entire life...

She's slept with men before, she mused. Not the ones in the line of duty, but random flings here and there. A couple stabs at building real relationships, a few dates that fizzled out into nothingness, but it all amounted to ashes in the end. There had been no trust or devotion, nothing bonding on an emotional level. Her sexuality had transformed to fit her merciless devotion to justice. How deeply ironic that the man who inspired that isolating hate and self-flagellation was also the first with whom she'd felt a real connection.

She'd felt bad for the men she slept with before, sure, but this was another beast entirely. There was nothing inherently erotic or sensual about this connection, but then again, she'd twisted and perverted those parts of her to the breaking point. Now, the core of her vulnerability was in the frayed memories of Tommy. How could she possibly deal with someone else who shared that same bond?

Annoyed and more than a little afraid of her own capacity to do something very regrettable, she extricated herself from the awkward embrace and rose from the bed. Without another look back, she made her way out of the room and into the kitchen. It was a small thing to refrain from stealing a glance to assess the tactical likelihood of him attacking her, but she decided that it was only fair to return the small gesture of trust.

Stuffed away in one of the cupboards, her latest unused burner was precisely where she'd left it last night. Pulling it out, she positioned herself in the corner opposite the door, leaning casually against the countertop but ensuring that Ashton could not sneak up on her, nor would he be able to see the screen if he happened to casually walk in. There was no conscious thought required for her decisions, only habits built up under the threat of death.

She tapped in the necessary code, then was left with nothing to do but wait. Inevitably, that led her to wonder whether Ashton might try to make a run for it. He couldn't reach the front door and thus the elevators without passing by the kitchen door, but it was possible that he could make a breakthrough one of the windows. Not that she particularly wanted him to throw his life away with a suicidal scheme like that, but if he did end up going that route, then she'd dramatically misunderstood his motivations and interest in taking down Ulrich.

Casey tapped her foot impatiently, but Carlisle was slow in replying. For a moment, she envisioned him playing with his kids and enjoying his bounty of meaningful human relationships, and she could feel nothing but envy. The feeling passed, less out of any personal magnanimity on her part and more because he was probably scribbling out details and orders for a dozen different operations after spending yet another night in the office. His family may be as living as hers was not, but in the end, both had a lonely duty to the public.

The phone buzzed in her hand, then the proper sequence of letters, numbers, and symbols scrolled by. The connection had been established, and she had fifteen minutes to correspond with headquarters.

UPDATE?

She stared at the standard query and wondered exactly what she was going to say. She'd come into the room with a vague idea that the mission parameters had changed, but she still didn't know exactly how. In the most logical and emotionless sense, she'd eliminated one suspect for a crime as cold as her heart and uncovered a dozen more. Did this mean she would have to recuse herself for being too close? Did it mean she had another tool at her disposal for taking down Ulrich? Did it even matter to the greater investigation?

FOUND ASHTON MALLICK, HE'S INNOCENT

Best to just stick to the basic facts. She couldn't figure out what to do with them, but maybe Carlisle could. She didn't necessarily always heed his guidance, but it had never gone unappreciated.

REPEAT AUTHENTICATION

In spite of herself, Casey chuckled. Yeah, she'd probably do the same thing in Carlisle's position. Getting that sort of message would undoubtedly lead one to believe that the agent in question had been compromised, either by having their brains addled or by having an external operative acquire their burner.

She tapped in the code once more. This time, Carlisle's response came much faster.

ARE YOU CERTAIN?

That was the problem, wasn't it? Her fingers hovered over the keys, her absolute stillness concealing the roiling questions in her head. How much did she trust Ashton? How far was she willing—

VIBRANT MIDNIGHT

Casey blinked. That couldn't be right. A general warning to abort the mission? No, but it was Carlisle, so she knew it was exactly what it looked like.

ULRICH SIGHTED IN THE AREA, EXTRACT IMMEDIATELY

All at once, a sudden calmness settled over Casey Anderson. She tapped back the expected reply, acknowledging and confirming that she was arranging extract. She lied easily even as she considered and reconsidered this wonderful bit of bounty.

It felt fairly easy to piece everything together. Perhaps Ulrich had missed one of his agents checking in, perhaps he'd been watching the area and noted their odd arrival, or maybe he was just in the area for other business. What mattered is that he was here, and now Casey could do something about it.

The only question was what.

Chapter 15

Ashton sat on the bed, feeling quite chilled but doing nothing about it. He could have wrapped himself up in blankets, could have burrowed deep under the covers to try to warm himself, but he knew that wouldn't help. This gripping, icy sensation was all on the inside.

He was awake and had been all along. That much was clear. In a way, that made things easier. In another, much more pressing way, it made things far worse.

The fact that he had unburned himself to someone else was a mild curative at best. He'd done it before, of course. He'd told his story a dozen times, a hundred times, to police officers, inmates, and anyone else who had listened. After that had added up to a heap of nothing, he'd slowly fallen into a pattern of closed lethargy that had lasted until last night. That he'd told the truth once more had felt good, but the lightening of his soul was only temporary. Already, he was feeling the crushing weight of obligation. Until he killed Ulrich, there would be no peace.

The problem, the real problem, was that he'd enjoyed himself too much. Was it possible to form an addiction after just one night? He didn't think so, but then again, that wasn't exactly what had happened, now was it? He hadn't found something new and completely novel last night, he'd just had a taste of something that he'd once had. Not the sex, but being close to another human being, allowing himself to be vulnerable in their presence, and maybe even sharing a fragment of trust. It wasn't anything he'd ever thought about before when he had it in abundance. Hell, he'd even gotten annoyed at Tommy for caring too much and butting in and telling him how to live his life. But now...

He heard her before he saw her. The prostitute swept into the room, wearing nothing more than a sheer robe. He hadn't paid much attention to what she had on earlier, but now he couldn't take his eyes off her. She didn't seem to feel the same way about him, for she headed straight to the window and stood on the tips of her toes to peer down.

Whatever she saw pleased her. With a grim smile, she turned back to Ashton and ran a hand sensuously down the curve of her breast.

"Do you recognize me?"

The words were so at odds with the motion that it took him a moment to process the question.

"I... yes, I know it wasn't a dream yet. You're the p— woman that I was with last night." His voice came out dry, so much so that he felt the need to lick his lips. It didn't escape his notice that she watched his tongue with avid interest.

She nodded slowly, advancing upon the bed and reaching down to untie the robe. There was so little fabric that it almost felt like she was getting less naked as she let the sheer, form-fitting fabric fall away, revealing only a brutally tempting set of lingerie. She wasn't near enough to touch, but still, his body shook in anticipation.

The prostitute arrived at a decision, and her expression of professional appeal fell away, replaced by a need so raw and essential that he nearly recoiled. She wasted no time ascending to the bed, then crawling towards him and pushing him back, back, and further back.

The animalistic lust emanating from her terrified Ashton. It felt like he wasn't even there. Anyone would do, he just happened to be the closest piece of meat that could satisfy her. That alone didn't bother him so much. The issue was that he could feel his body responding in kind, craving to be devoured by such a huntress.

"Why?" he asked, but the question died on his lips as she forced a kiss. Deep, draining, and aggressive, she demanded more and more of him, driving him down to the bed as she leaned down to devour him. Her hands weren't even touching him, but it felt like she was violently scratching him with rakes of her nails.

Why indeed? Feeling very nearly divorced from his body, he could not help but wonder why? It wasn't so much a question of why this woman was doing what she was doing. On some level, he perfectly understood why someone might want to have a little animalistic rutting from time to time. That didn't bother him.

What did bother him was the way that he desperately craved her. It went beyond simply wanting sexual release. It went beyond desiring a partner in bed that could tend to your needs. It spoke to a deeper need that he'd never even realized, a yearning to be punished and destroyed, to be taken by someone that had so little regard for him that his sins didn't even matter. It wasn't a show of tenderness that his scarred soul needed but a display of savagery that made his cock harder than it had ever been before.

Clearly, he wasn't the only one who realized that. She pressed down upon him, grinding the silk of her crotch against his own. His cock was still restrained by his underwear, running straight up his body. Far from reaching down to free it and leap to the main event, she slid back and forth, his cock against her lips with two layers of fabric to deaden the sensations just enough to prevent an accident.

From the window, there came a loud crashing sound from down below. Both froze for just an instant, then Ashton hugged her, holding her tight, pulling her down, and demanding that she continue to ravage him.

The prostitute had no interest in him taking control. Her hands moved to his forearms, pulling them out above his head, putting all of her weight atop him. Her legs were splayed wide across his crotch but folded back so that her feet curled around his knees. A twisting, sinuous struggle for dominance, she jerked against him, shuddering and shaking above.

He looked up as she pulled away from a kiss. Her eyes were shut tight, her eyelashes fluttering in concentration and pleasure. She bit her lip, which compelled him to reach up and brush a finger along that inviting wetness, but her immobilization of him was complete. He could do nothing but wait for her pleasure.

Or perhaps not nothing. He could still rise at the hips, meeting her and imparting some generosity. It felt unfair to be the object of her masturbation and to do nothing at all to help, or so his frazzled sense of chivalry demanded.

At his modest offering, she arched her back and frozen, statuesque above him, her throat bared as she looked up to the ceiling. As to whatever the expression on her face may have been, he couldn't even begin to guess. On any other day, with any other woman, he would have imagined unabashed pleasure, but that didn't feel quite right.

"I hope you don't take this the wrong way," she said unsteadily, her voice ragged. "But this is for my benefit, not yours." Ashton surpassed a laugh as he heard the words that he'd spoken yesterday repeated back to him.

Ashton had no thought of complaining. In fact, he didn't have much time to think anything at all before she was upon him once more, cascading down and gliding across until she was wholly between his legs, her forearms resting on his thighs as her ass waggled back and forth in the air. She looked at him with a hungry, teasing expression in her eyes, and he knew that she would gain just as much pleasure from his re-actions as her actions, if not more.

Her hand slipped beneath his underwear, lifting the sweaty stickiness and letting a tiny breeze in. He realized be-latedly that it had to be her breath upon him. Fingers quested around his shaft, greedily moving up to touch the tip and see just how much of a mess he'd made prematurely. When she found only the tiny drop that came standard, her tiny purr shook every bone in his body.

Ashton had thought himself fairly experienced when it came to what pleased him. Granted, most of that had been a result of his introduction into BDSM in his late teens, plus it had been more than a few years in the past. All told, he had a very outdated mental image of what his own body's pleasure looked like, and all of it exploded in an instant when her teeth closed teasingly on his thigh flesh.

It was a tiny, soft nip, but the way her wet heat radiated out at the same time that her fingers curled around his man-hood resulted in a combination too dangerous to bear. He moaned without shame but didn't even think for a moment of bringing his hands down to run through her hair. As surely as if she was still pinning him down, Ashton was in her web now.

"I don't want you to think I've changed my mind," she said conversationally between playful caresses with her tongue. "This is still all for my pleasure."

"Clearly," was all he could manage before her hand squeezed.

It was a remarkable feat of logistics, the way that she had one hand sliding under one leg of his underwear while also juggling her oral teasing and edging her other hand up to approach from the opposite side. Slow, steady pumps with one hand while the other brushed up a little further south, carefully cupping his testicles. Her lips moved closer, then further away, giving no hint as to when she would be offering final release.

Or would he even get to enjoy a final release? The thought that she might enjoy tormenting him had crossed his mind. It was a testament to the shattered state of his self-understanding that he didn't even question how the idea of deserving torture intersected with his sexuality, but it certainly made him hard.

And then she was moving in for the kill, pulling down his underwear to bare his skin to the world. He'd been naked before, but he'd never felt quite this exposed. The way she looked down at his cock was enough to make him seriously entertain the possibility that she wanted to eat him up, body and soul.

Transfixed, he craned his neck to watch as her tongue ran tiny circles around her lips, imbuing them with a natural red glossiness that could put any lipstick to shame. Plump and tantalizing, her kiss fell slowly upon his stiff cock. Then, he saw only white.

It wasn't such a bad thing to experience purely by touch and sound. To feel himself bucking and rising to meet her, to be forced back down with the slightest pressure. She demanded that he remain still and quivering while she caressed, sucked, and licked the very tip of his cock, all at the same time. It was a swirling and heady experience, threatening to drag him straight to the edge. How could she manage so much with so little?

The answer was obvious. It was her job to do this, but that didn't explain it completely. That she would be adept at quickly finishing the job and collecting a paycheck was one thing, but she said she was doing this for herself. Did she enjoy making men climax quickly and with what amounted to little more than a chaste kiss in the grand scheme of sexuality?

It made sense, he decided as she went deeper, swallowing him inch by inch and never so much as gagging. He would probably enjoy getting women off quickly, but at the same time, if it was his job, then he might not think the same way. There was really no way that he could grasp her thoughts and feelings, just as he knew that nobody else on the planet could grasp his own struggles and suffering. It was intimacy as fragile and fleeting as the string of spit connecting him to her as she pulled away with a deep flush on her cheeks.

She looked up to him, lips parted just enough to let her cute little panting continue. Her entire body gently heaved with the past exertion, and if he just lifted his legs, he could surely feel her breasts against him. But he did not because he was not the one in control here.

He thought it couldn't get any more intense, but he was wrong. She twisted her head back and forth, swirling her tongue from side to side, and the contradiction pulled a rattling gasp from his lips.

"Fuck, don't stop," he pleaded, expecting absolutely nothing of the sort. A large part of him was hoping that she'd deny him, not because he wanted to cum, but because the idea of being overpowered and having his will denied was intoxicating.

A dull thud echoed from somewhere below in the building. He didn't notice, but she certainly did. The prostitute pulled away, her eyes hazy with pleasure and her mouth dripping with spit and a little something extra. She wiped it away with a finger, pulling the strands down to cover and wet his slick, shining cock.

Her hands clung to him, her nails digging into his skin as she pulled herself higher and higher, gliding against him, bare skin alternating with impossibly soft underwear. Her breasts washed over his belly, then his chest. A hand reached down to slip her panties to the side, and then he could feel liquid fire against his cock.

He couldn't take it anymore. He had to kiss her. He needed to have her, but her hold over him was irresistible, and so he didn't move a muscle save to tremble.

Bit by bit, she pushed herself up until he was staring into her glorious breasts, jutting out from a gracefully arched back. She looked to the ceiling, basking in the stretch before rising to allow him entry.

"Tell me," she said as she slowly looked down at him, her eyes alight, "what would you do if you saw Ulrich?"

He didn't have a single second to think about it before she was sinking onto him, taking him entirely within herself. His body and hers were merged, the warm tightness of her pussy not offering even the slightest resistance. The walls were only there to guide and caress him, to invite him to share intimacy that not only had he not known in the last decade, but that he'd never truly known. He'd had sex before, but he'd never had this.

His lips moved without conscious thought, answering her even as his eyes slid shut. "I would kill him."

One jerking motion, and she was seated atop him, sheathing him entirely. He was so deep inside her, and he almost never wanted to move again. But only almost.

She rocked back and forth, slowly at first, not allowing the pumping motion that he so craved. Back and forth, the bed creaking, their thighs slippery against one another, drops of sweat coursing down her body to land atop him and mingle with his own. He could even feel the exact softness of the panties parted to his side against his leg. Never had he been so perfectly aware of a moment, nor did he imagine he ever would be again.

And then, just for a single flash of an instant, he thought he saw Tommy's face above him. As quickly as the macabre sight crossed his mind, it was gone.

Seeming to sense his thoughts, the escort paused, only to press herself down to his chest, bringing her nose only a hair away from his own. Her eyes drilled down into his, her crotch completely still against his own.

His blood boiled as the compulsion to confess his guilt warred with the need for release, and the desire to be overwhelmed contrasted with the urge to thrust up into her.

She searched one eye, then the other. Her gaze was cold and merciless, completely at odds with how flushed her cheeks were and how she panted in exertion. Sweat rolled down from her hairline to her chin, where it quivered on the precipice, not quite forming a drop to fall the short distance between them. It could not bridge the gap.

A crash sounded below, followed by some shouting. He had no idea whether it died down or not, for his attention was entirely on the way she turned her head and dipped down to press her cheek against his. Her lips pressed upon his ear, worrying the flesh, licking, kissing, breathing.

"Everything will be alright, but only if you fuck me as hard as you can."

Thoughts didn't travel quite as fast as primal instinct unleashed. All at once, Ashton reached down to grab a handful of ass, holding her tight against him, and thrust up into her, lifting all her weight up with a mighty groan.

She moaned into his ear, a wickedly high-pitched sound that he didn't imagine her capable of. The force of her breath made him tremble even as it deafened him. His grip grew tighter, and his wild bucking lost all semblance of rhythm. No conscious thought was involved, just all the savage force he could muster with her body bearing down on him. She jiggled and bounced atop him, a testament to his strength that pushed him past the boundaries of usual exhaustion. Over and over, higher and higher, with less and less technique, he fucked the whore that had tried to dominated him. There was no way in hell he'd let that happen again. He'd do exactly what she'd said she wanted but on his terms.

"Did you— oh fuck..." she half-whispered, half cried into his ear. He could feel the passion in her voice, feel the vibrations that he was sending through her. "Did you lie to me earlier?"

It was an odd question, but nothing that could distract him from his taking her hard and fast. He rolled to the side, not even bothering to take her from above. His legs tangled with hers, and he jerked against her, into her, as buoyed by the new sense of weightlessness as he was dragged down by the exertion so far.

"What?" he groaned, compelled as he was to do exactly what she asked, and if that meant that he was going to answer her questions, then he would damn well answer as best he could. Bit hard when he had no idea what the question actually meant though.

"Everything you... fuck yes, keep doing that. Everything you said earlier, was any of it a lie?"

Even with his mind as filled as it was by primal longing, he could still sense the wrongness of that question. Why was she asking him such a question? Was she doing this all because she worked for Ulrich? If so, he could deal with that after. He just had to finish first, nothing else mattered.

"No," he said with a particularly harsh thrust of his hips. If he'd wanted her to cringe away in pain, he was sorely disappointed. If he'd rather wanted her to moan appreciatively and cling to him all the harder, then he was rewarded and then some.

"Good," she whispered through slitted eyes.

The front door crashed open.

Chapter 16

For a frozen instant, Casey watched as Ashton Malick was torn between two extremes. In his eyes, there was a dawning horror and surprise as he realized that someone had just burst into the apartment. His body, however, was perfectly happy to continue thrusting away like a rutting animal. She was enjoying it well enough, or at least as much as someone could in her position.

The chorus of male voices from the hallway quickly materialized into three figures that surprised her not a bit. Two men stood dressed in black, looking so ghoulish, unintelligent, and cruel that they must have been competing against one another to see who could look the most stereotypical.

Between them was a man that would be seared into her memory as long as she lived. She'd looked through a thousand photographs of him a thousand times each, and the square, neatly bearded, shaved head only got more unappealing each time she'd looked. He held himself with absolute self-assurance, knowing himself to be the most powerful person in the room at all times.

She took them in with a single glance, never stopping her wild and reckless embrace with Ashton. It was a bold plan that she had settled upon, perhaps even a stupid plan, but it relied on believing Ulrich to be an overconfident son of a bitch, and that had never steered her wrong so far.

The three men had known what was going on in the bedroom before they stepped through the doorway, of course. She'd made damn sure of that with her loud whimpering moans. The irony was not lost on her that she likely didn't even need to have perfected the art of making natural, animalistic moans of pleasure. These brutes had likely never heard anything other than a faked orgasm in their lives.

"Well, well, well, what do we have here?" Ulrich asked in his deep, sensuous voice. "Is that..."

It was the moment everything came down to. Casey nestled herself against the body at her side even as it slowed to a stop. Ashton hadn't had any warning and was still processing the shock, but that was the only way to make it look real on such short notice.

"Ashton Malick, as I live and breathe!" Ulrich bellowed out, with his goons laughing humorlessly along.

He hadn't recognized Casey, and that was all that mattered. If he had — and he surely had moles that likely provided him with the identities of undercover government agents — then he would be on edge. Instead, he thought he'd just discovered one of his wayward employees stepping out of line and rutting like an animal.

"Take her outside." The command was given with no more enthusiasm than an order to take out the trash.

Hands settled upon her, big meaty appendages that sharply contrasted with Ashton's decidedly skilled fingers. Lifted to her feet, she was then promptly dragged out of the room, but not before squeezing Ashton and accomplice's hand. She didn't dare look at his face for fear of anything being given away. For now, she just had to trust that he could handle his end of the equation.

As she was manhandled to the kitchen, she went over the various cupboards and where she'd hidden a selection of tools, both lethal and otherwise. It was more a calming exercise than anything else. Casey was quite sure that she had her half of the situation well in hand.

There wasn't a snowball's chance in hell that she was actually going to learn the names of the two men with her, and the chances of her caring were even smaller, so she elected to label them Handsy and Handsier.

Once they were completely in the kitchen, they closed the door, then stood in front of it for good measure, leering down at her with completely naked lust in their eyes.

"Never seen one of those before?" Handsy laughed, reaching down to grotesquely stroke the front of his pants.

Handsier laughed at the unfortunate attempt at a joke but didn't mirror the gesture. On re-examining the question, she wondered if she may have gotten their names mixed up.

"So, which one of you is first?" Casey sighed gustily. She tried to appear as bored and unseductive as was possible, which was a relatively simple affair in the straight-backed kitchen chairs.

The grins on their faces flickered as if they weren't quite expecting her to actually offer anything. Fortunately — or rather, unfortunately — she was pretty familiar with this sort of false bravado.

"Hurry up now. We don't have all day," she said with a loud sniff.

Uncertainly, Handsy, the ex-Handsier, stepped forward and cautiously began to undo his belt. Casey had first thought that it was a bit counterintuitive, but if one took the initiative, they could play a great role in guiding exactly how the encounter went. A man might walk into a situation thinking to take whatever pleasures he might, the woman's wants be damned. Still, if the woman sets the tone by offering something lesser, then the man might accept and not dare to ask anything more. Unfortunately for this pair, they were about to learn just how much "lesser" her services were.

He slapped his pathetic excuse for a cock down into her expectant hand. It wasn't a terrible grotesque thing, Casey contemplated as she looked at it. She found it rather distasteful to judge people for things outside their control, after all. Hygiene, however, was completely within the control of Handsy, and on that count, he left more than a little to be desired.

Still, it was easy enough to start tugging away. With a lazy pace and a bored expression, she looked up at the man towering over her. He was breathing out of his mouth, which was about par for the course, but then again, perhaps that was also something he was born with and couldn't help.

"You too, come on," she called to Handsier, who was rubbing his fingers against his cock his trousers. Yeah, she had the names right now.

In short order, she was tugging on a pair of mostly clean cocks, one in each hand. Thankfully, putting them near her mouth was nowhere near on the table, and it wasn't just because of any personal disgust involved. God knows that if you put your head down there, men can't keep from sticking their hands all over you and trying to take control. No, best keep them at a distance and not egg them on too much.

All except Ashton, she mused, changing up the pace and beating their pudding a tad faster. The pair acted like it was the most glorious sexual experience they'd ever received, their heads lolling back and gasping as they received painfully substandard handjobs.

Actually, after taking a look at their hands and the meaty fingers they had, perhaps it was the best manual stimulation they'd had in a while. The simple touch of slim fingers was probably enough to get them off.

There was definitely another, much bigger aspect to the whole thing, though. Have one guy, and maybe he'll make his desires known, maybe not. Have an experience with two straight guys trying to outcompete one another in masculinity, and then neither will want to lose face by saying anything.

These were the kind of thoughts that kept Casey occupied while she wondered what exactly was going on in the other room. No noises were coming from out there, but she knew that had far more to do with the soundproofing of the apartment than the nature of the conversation. By her estimate, Ulrich would be mocking Ashton. Hopefully, Ashton had already found the gun that she'd left by his side. If not...

"God, that feels so good," Handsy muttered. Or maybe that was Handsier.

"Alright, let's get down to business," Casey grunted, slipping down from the chair to kneel on the floor. She edged forward just enough that she was right between the men, with one on each side. They both looked down at her with such leering lust in their eyes that she stifled a laugh. Well, at least she had no compunctions about these guys deserving it. Nobody this dumb could complain about what came next.

Now, if these guys had just unzipped and pulled out, things might be a little harder, but since they'd both completely dropped trou, her job could not be any easier. Thus, when she suddenly released them and reached further back, simultaneously going for two scrotums, there was nothing whatsoever in her way. With an iron grip, she choked the life out of two pairs of balls.

Typically, this would have been incredibly painful but not enough to settle the matter entirely. However, with these two blokes so close to one another, their natural responses to double over in pain resulted in a cracking collision of heads that made even Casey wince. It wasn't enough for her to bother checking on their vitals once they crashed down to the ground and took a few more knocks, but it was enough to feel slightly bad about it all.

Casey then crept out of the kitchen after arming herself with a sidearm hidden among the cereal boxes in the pantry. She moved down the hallway and peeked around the corner, only to find that Ashton was sitting nearly naked on the bed, gasping for air and staring at nothing. Ulrich was slumped down on the ground, now sporting a shiny red hole in the middle of his forehead,

"Wow," Casey murmured, unable to refrain from scratching her head.

Ashton looked up, seeing her for the first time. His eyes were bloodshot as his face twisted in a rictus grin of panic. "I didn't... you have to... he was going to kill me."

Casey nodded, looking back down at the body. "Yeah, no, I can see that. I was just impressed at the soundproofing. I didn't even hear the shot!"

Chapter 17

Ashton stared at the blank white wall in front of him. He'd been sitting alone for what felt like an eternity, but he had no idea if it had been five minutes or five days. Everything all seemed so dreamlike now. Maybe he'd never woken up at all. Maybe he'd broken out of prison, stolen that car, and promptly crashed. That would make more sense than what his brain was trying to tell him had happened.

The door clicked open, then she walked in. Definitely not a prostitute, he now decided. Not unless prostitutes usually worked as undercover agent as well. In a smart suit, she was completely unrecognizable compared to the goddess of lust that had demanded so much from him... this morning? Had it really been less than a day?

"Ashton Malick," she said as she took a seat across from him. The desk was as lifeless as the rest of the room, and she was so at odds with it that he could scarcely believe she was real.

"Who are you?" he asked, his throat raspy. "I killed Ulrich."

She tapped her fingers and stared at him with such intensity that he was left without any doubts as to whether this was the same woman.

"You did kill Ulrich. He's dead, and a lot of people probably like to pat you on the back for that. A lot of people would also want to kill you for that, so I'd keep that in mind before bragging about anything."

Ashton laughed, but the sound barely came out as more than hoarse creaking. The idea that he would brag about this was beyond the pale.

"And I'm Casey Anderson," she added, leaning back in her chair. Then, she just waited.

He stared at her for a time, unsure if that was supposed to mean something. He wanted to ask if she was with the FBI, but something nagged at him, and he couldn't quite put his finger on it. This was all probably in his imagination, and it didn't matter anyway, but...

Anderson. Oh no.

He looked at her once again, taking in the entirety of her face this time. She looked nothing like him. Not even a little bit. The problem was that she looked just like that spindly, smiling little girl that had followed Tommy around everywhere. The kid sister was all grown up, and the smiles were a lot colder now. She'd filled out marvelously, but even thinking that felt wrong and disturbing.

Ashton very nearly retched but caught himself at the last moment. "What... how..."

She took pity on him, leaning forward enough to push a cup of water in his direction. She folded her arms on the table, unable to completely suppress her raw sex appeal but doing a decent job anyway.

"It's not a particularly complicated story, Ashton. I wasn't a particularly imaginative girl, and I certainly had my share of the family stubbornness, so after Tommy was killed, I decided to do something about it. Turns out that 'doing something about it took a lot longer than I expected, and before I could blink, I was making a career out of it. I am sure that me sticking to it for so long had a lot to do with the irritation of not being able to find one bastard in particular."

"Me." There was nothing else to say. How could he even begin to apologize to this girl?

"You," she said with a mirthless smile. "But here we are, and everything is put right. My brother is avenged, the guilty party has been suitably punished, and an innocent man walks free."

"I'm not innocent," was all he could say before his cheeks heated at the memories of what he'd done to her. Oh God, Tommy's sister. How could he not have known?

"No," she agreed. "You did do a few things wrong, which I know does weigh heavily on your conscience. However, by my reckoning, as well as the reckoning of everyone who matters, you've already paid for those minor infractions several times over. As of now, you and the law are more or less square."

He stared at her, not daring to hope.

"I... what do I do?"

She looked at him for a time, leaving him wondering if his question had been too inane. It certainly sounded so to his ears, but he couldn't find the worse to clarify.

"It's a good question. You've been out of polite society for a long time. There are also going to be a lot of people that want to hurt you as revenge. It's not like NYPD will admit to having you previously employed, and I'm quite sure you don't have any money to your name. Quite a bind you've found yourself in, Mr. Malick."

Every new point was like a pinprick. She was right. This wasn't a dream. This was a nightmare. He'd wanted to take out Ulrich, but what about after that? He'd never given a single thought to how he would survive.

Casey took out something from a manilla envelope, sliding it across the table to join the untouched water. It was a business card of some sort.

"What's this?" he asked dully, all hope vanished.

"The bureau is always looking out for interesting hires," she said with a raised eyebrow. "Based on your interview, I'd say you did pretty well."

"Interview?"

Slowly, she licked her lips and tossed him a flirty wink. "What, did you think all that was just for fun? First rule: everyone's got an ulterior motive, all the time."

"And what's the second rule?" he asked before he could stop himself.

"Join up and find out. It's not like you've got anything better to do."

Ashton Mallick watched as Casey Anderson got up and strolled out of the room. Somehow, he got the feeling it wouldn't be the last he was seeing of her.

Excerpt from Married Games

By J.F. Lowe

Prologue

As the prisms of light filter through our bedroom door, the sound of my husband's light snore beside me bears no comfort. I'm exhausted, but I don't want to close my eyes. It's not that I am afraid. Or maybe I am. But not of my husband, god no. He is the most loving, supportive and caring man I have ever met. I know he loves me and I am completely and utterly head over heels in love with Matthew. He is the kind of man that I always wished I could have my happily ever after with.

So what had happened? Why I am I laying here wondering what had put me in the hospital? Why had four Victorian Police officers come and searched my house and threaten to take my husband away? Why did I feel like something seriously wrong had occurred? I just don't know. I know that exhaustion is playing its part.

I watch the rise and fall of my husband's chest; maybe if I concentrate on that, I will fall into a lull and drift off to sleep. But after another hour somehow it's not as comforting as it once was. Instead, my chest feels tight, and my heart continues to race. I force myself to take a deep breath, but the anxiety rises once again. I know something is wrong. Is it me? Did I do something? Did I take something? The emergency doctor had told me my blood alcohol was 0.02. which to me was no that high. With that amount of alcohol in my system, I could still have legally driven a motor vehicle.

We had two bottles of wine between the two of us. A bottle of crisp white Sauvignon Blanc and I had barely finished my first glass of the Shiraz. It had been a typical Saturday night. In fact, it was the first Saturday night in months that we had decided to stay in, have a few wines and a nice cheese platter. Cheese and wine had always been our thing. The cheese platter had had all of his favourites: a beautiful Tasmanian blue, a creamy triple Brie and apricot and almond cheese, topped off with my favourite Danish salami and a line of plain and peppered crackers on each side of the board. We even had our favourite YouTube playlist running on the television in the lounge room as background noise.

So, why did I end up in hospital? Why did the police come? And why did I feel like our lives have just been turned upside down? I lay watching my husband. No, it definitely isn't fear of my husband keeping me awake but maybe more fear of myself. A sinking feeling that I may have just ruined my marriage, my life, and hurt the only man I have ever truly loved.

Chapter 1

Sarah

Three Months Earlier...

The keys turn in the front door. He's home, my love is home. It's only been eight hours since I last saw him, but each day seems to feel longer. I sit waiting to greet him as he enters our inner-city five-bedroom penthouse apartment. As the jingle of the keys play, nothing sounded better than to know he was home. I was not alone anymore. Except for Baxter, that is. Baxter our little fur baby, a little seven-month-old Jack Russel that from the moment we went to the breeders home he came right out and licked my foot as if a sign to say, you're my human.

I am his human alright, he absolutely ignores all others when it comes to taking orders. He is a people dog, but I am the only he will listen to when I tell him to sit or no, or basically any other command. Then again, I am the only one that he spends all his days with, as he sits by my feet while I either write or read—that's where life has come to in my thirty-six-year long life. I turned into everything I never thought I would be.

Gone were the days where I was a CEO of a multi-million dollar company, living the high life on cruise ships travelling the world and earning a good salary as I went. My life was now isolation, novel characters and wine.

My husband finally enters our apartment. You would never think that he is a construction mogul the way he places his filthy construction lunch box on the kitchen table. Then again, Matthew is always the hands-on kind of guy. He knows every part of his business inside and out. He still gets on the tools most days, changing out of his suit and into his high vis gear before helping out on-site when needed.

Mr Reliable is what I called him when we first met. Just like his routine every day when he gets home from work. He kisses me hello before heading to the veranda and disposing of his finished lemonade bottle in the bottle recycling bin. It is the same for his lunch and pretty much everything about my husband. His alarm goes off at five-thirty, we both get up. He opens the wardrobe and dresses in his suit for work, and I head off to make his lunch. It's the same every week, every week-day. Two ham and cheese wraps with three snack size chocolates and a 1.25 litre bottle of sugar-free lemonade. I used to think that anybody that ate the same thing each day must be a bit strange because to have the same monotonous thing would be like eating cardboard.

That was the thing though, ever since meeting my husband two years ago, it was always the same. Every week-day was the same, and when he returned home at night, it was more of the same. After he returns from the veranda, he kisses me lightly again before retreating to the shower. I had the same routine too. While he showered, I would get up and grab a glass of wine and sit on the couch until six o'clock, when the news starts. I would then rise from the couch and begin making dinner.

Day after day during the week, nothing changes and the weekend is always just as predictable. Saturday morning breakfast out at our local cafe, caramel latte and smashed avocado on toast for me and either pancakes or corn fritters if he was feeling adventurous. After, we would go and see an elderly neighbour who had been placed in a nursing home by her children, and then we would either go the local bar or head to a restaurant before heading to the bar later in the evening.

Our lives are the same story week after week, like the same song on repeat. The only change we had in our lives was a recent diagnosis of cancer for me. A lump that had appeared in my mouth a month before our wedding had grown and now was creating issues with my speech. not to mention being ridiculously annoying as it rubs against my teeth.

I had thought it was a simple mouth ulcer. Something that would disappear after the stress of the wedding had died down. But it hadn't, and eventually, I got sick of it and went to my local doctor. It took her less than five minutes to refer me to the Ear, Nose and Throat specialist on a priority list, and less than ten days later the cancers were surgically removed.

It was another blow to my health, something that I had to fight with since the early months of my life. Another cancer. Another surgery and another time in my life where the worry of making it to my next birthday begins. It was something I thought about regularly. It feels like I'm a living and breathing medical book. I had already learnt how to cope after my second cancer diagnosis six years earlier, but this time I had my husband by my side at every step. That was something I was not used to. I was used to being alone throughout the process.

Doctors, chemotherapy, radiation and what seemed like never-ending moments of being a pin cushion. Throughout my first two cancers, my former husband was never there, nor any family or friends. I had been sent to the hospital seven hours away in the capital city, and my former sister-in-law sat in the waiting area on the ground floor each and every time I went. But that was always the case.

I became chatty with the medical professionals along the way just to keep myself from crying for each procedure. I had developed such a habit that I was on a first-name basis with my local phlebotomists at the pathology lab. We made light of the fact that I was there on either a weekly or daily basis, depending on the circumstances. I called her my very own vampire. She laughed when I said she was more real than Edward from the Twilight Saga. Then again, maybe she didn't realise that at the time I just wanted to be immortal, or at least be alive long enough to watch my three children grow up, get married and maybe one day make me a grandmother, but I never told her that.

This time though I wasn't alone. Matthew sat beside me, holding my hand and gently rubbing my back as we waited in the admission section of the hospital. I'm not sure who was more scared and whether he was holding my hand to console me or if it made him feel better, as he didn't speak. I'm not quite sure that he could. He had become more animated from the moment I told him that I had cancer. That day played through my head.

I sat patiently in the specialist's office and told myself that I might walk away with a few stitches today as surely he would just lance what I thought was a cyst. After the stitches dissolved, I would be back to normal.

That wasn't the case. After a careful examination and nasal camera scan the specialist, who had been all smiles at the beginning of the appointment, had become sullen. He was extremely polite, but I could tell that he was trying to find the words to say to me it wasn't as simple as I thought. Letting out a deep breath, I'm sure he had been holding.

"Sarah, we need to take this out and immediately" he said, flipping through his leather-bound desk diary.

"I am going to move some things around, but I will book the surgery for the morning of the eighteenth. There is no waiting for this and, to be honest, the severity of it won't be completely clear until I open it up and can do further exploration under general anaesthetic." He raised his head to finally look at my face.

"Umm, what am I missing here. I thought this was just an ulcer or a cyst that would be over and done with today. "

"Sarah, I believe what you have is mucoepidermoid carcinoma. Which is a form of cancer that affects the salivary glands. We need to do surgery and straight away."

Bile rose in my throat, cancer. No. Not again. I had already beaten cancer twice - first Ewing's sarcoma in my right humerus in 2009 and then medullary carcinoma in my right breast in 2013. It can't be cancer, I can not go through that again. The doctor's voice was drowned out by the sound of my heart pounding through my head.

My heart raced, and my stomach continued to churn while the rest of my body seemed to be on autopilot. It must have been because I managed to leave the ear, nose and throat specialist and drive the 35 minutes through the city home before the tears finally began to fall.

"Sarah. Sarah." A shaking on my thigh brought me back to the present.

"Sarah, the nurse is here to take you to pre-op" my husband offered his hand to help me from my seat.

"Oh, I'm sorry." I stood, collecting my bag. I turned and gave my husband a kiss before following the nurse through the restricted access area.

Chapter 2

Matthew

I had known that I was all wrong for her, that I never should have touched her, but I'd been so drawn to her sweet innocence, her genuine smiles, her interest in me as a person, that I'd been unable to resist her.

She made me laugh when I'd forgotten how. She made me want to be more when I'd stopped believing in anything good. She'd pulled me out of a grim existence and had given me something to hope for. She'd made me feel when I thought my father's physical and verbal abuse had stripped me of the ability to care for anyone or anything.

She was my salvation, my reason for turning my life around when I had been so close to not giving a shit about anything. I probably would have turned out just like my old man if it hadn't been for her giving me something to truly live for.

I had been stuck in a rut of work, sex and booze. My longtime friend Eden had been the only constant in my life, but even then, our relationship was toxic. We had met at a BDSM club in Melbourne's outer suburbs after I'd received an invitation from a childhood buddy that had gone into the Navy. He and his mates owned the club and offered me a place to relax and learn the lifestyle.

The moment I met Eden, I knew he was trouble, but I couldn't help but look at him with a sense of awe. The way that women seemed to flock to him. He was charismatic, and, from what I had learnt, a good dominant. It was only when I walked past one of the view rooms one evening that I learnt that he was a man that also liked to share women. I stopped by the window watching him as he, in unison with another man, fucked the woman fifty shades of Sunday. It was one of the most erotic things I had ever seen. It was at that moment Eden's eyes locked with mine, and his silent nod became the start of a long friendship.

We shared many women over the next five years, some as one night stands and others more long term. None of them stayed though. They always ended up telling me that they only really wanted Eden. So I was back to being alone. That was until the day I met Sarah.

She had sent through a request to the construction company I worked for at the time for a quote on bathroom renovations on her inner-city apartment. I had turned up early as usual and grabbed a coffee before heading up to her apartment. When I arrived, the door had been slightly ajar. I knocked but no answer. I called out but no response. I stepped into the apartment, and that's when I saw her. Headphones on in front of her laptop, in an oversized white shirt, apparently braless, and wearing the most granny-like underwear I think I had ever seen. She was the most gorgeous woman I had ever seen.

Her foot was tapping away to whatever she was listening to, which made her breast bounce. I couldn't help but stare. I watched as she picked up her glass of water absentmindedly before missing her mouth completely and spilling it down her front. She jumped from her chair.

I couldn't help myself. I had to laugh. She was the sexiest and clumsiest person I'd ever seen. It must be my laugh that alerted her to the fact she wasn't alone. When she turned, she shrieked. My mouth went dry, and I was instantly hard. It was like the wet T-shirt competition of my dreams—the beautiful full globes on full display through the wet shirt. I stepped back with my hands up to show I wasn't going to hurt her or was some creepy stalker.

"I'm sorry, the door was open. I'm Matthew Davidson, I have an appointment to quote on the bathroom" I stammered.

It was then she seemed to remember that she was half-naked, trying to cover herself with her hands. No matter how much she tried to cover, the wet shirt showed everything, but I wasn't exactly going to point that out because I'm sure if she looked at me properly she would have noticed the tent in my pants.

"Oh, shit. That's today," she finally said.

"Yes, eleven o'clock," I replied, trying to hide my amusement at the scene in front of me.

"Umm, can you give me a minute? I'll be right back" she turned and disappeared.

That was the day I knew Sarah would one day become my wife.

Two years later, she did. Now we were both successful in our own right. Sarah, with her training company and then a Best Seller novelist. I had landed on my feet after meeting her, seeing that anything is possible no matter what crap cards life had given you as a child. A shiver of horror ran through me at the thought of my childhood. My father had abused my mother, and by the time I was eight, he had decided that I was fair game too. That was until the day he finally went too far and killed my mother by throwing her into a wall one too many times and received a life sentence for murder.

God, I wish my mother had the strength that my wife did. My wife never gave up, she just grinned and said that only the good die young and there was no way cancer would stop her. Matthew sighed; it may not kill her, but this being her third cancer certainly is taking its toll.

Initially, we had thought nothing of it. It was just a small lump that we thought was an ulcer that showed up about the same time as her mother did for our wedding. She laughed it off, saying, "I'm glad it's only a mouth ulcer and not a stomach ulcer because spending a week with my mother is bound to give anyone an ulcer."

After that, we thought nothing of it. It was only when her speech slowly started to change that she finally went to the doctors. Now I'm sitting in the family waiting room until she finishes surgery.

I got up from my seat again and started pacing. Why is this taking so long? It's been two hours already, and they said she would be out by now. I check my phone. Nope, nothing. No calls from recovery and no one had come out to get me yet. As I stride up to the nurse's desk, the nurse holds her hand up me.

"Mr Davidson, it has only been a few minutes since you last asked, I don't have any news yet. I will let you know when I have information. Please take a seat. Or better yet, the hospital cafe is just down the hall if you would like something. I will come and get you if something changes."

"Fine" I grunt before turning towards the hall. I needed a distraction, a project.

*****

"Eden, how are you? I was wondering if you could do me a favour. I'm looking for a new car for my wife."

"Ah the illustrious Sarah, I am yet to meet. I would have met her at your wedding if you hadn't eloped"

"Yeah, yeah you knew why she said she would do anything to keep things from the press and her mother." I said this in jest, but it was partly true the press had been following them since they had been listed as Melbourne's new power couple.

Her mother was a handful, but nothing compared to his family.

"So, what's on the cards my friend, something sporty fun to ride like the old days? Or are you a kept man these days and need practical?"

"Actually, I'm thinking the latest Mazda CX-8, if you have any on hand. I'd like to have it in the next week or two." Not that I was telling him, but I was hoping it would become a family car for us as my work dual cab ute wasn't exactly suitable for a baby seat. I never thought I would be thinking about having a child of my own, but that was Sarah. She gave me hope of having a family that I never had. I looked at my watch again, and another fifteen minutes had passed. I need to find out what the hell was taking so long with Sarah's operation.

"Look mate I have to get going, flick me through an email with model details and colour." I wasn't sharing with Eden what was happening. Him further involved in our lives could only end one way. I brushed the errant thoughts of Eden aside as I stalked back to the nurse's desk.

Series by J.F. Lowe

Masters of Highclere:
A Sailors Daughter
Coxswains Cuffs
Returning to Highclere
Medical Ménage
Masters of Highclere Forbidden Stories (Standalone)

Love Games:
Married Games
Revenge Games
Sinful Games
Connor (Love Games Trilogy - Novella)

Protecting Her Innocence (Standalone)

Jealous - Not Me! (Standalone)

Composing Sins
Recording Sins

Seducing Series:
Seducing Austin
Seducing Vegas (Coming 2021)
Seducing Philly (Coming 2021)

Tis The Season For Romance - Anthology

Road to Love Series (Coming 2021):
Broken Love
Departed Love
Forbidden Love

About J.F. Lowe

I grew up in a country town in Central Queensland, Australia. As the fruit of a long line of military men and not much to do, it gave me plenty of time to create a fantasy world full of hot men and wild romances. It was only when I met my own hot alpha that I decided to share my love of books and writing with the world.

Nowadays, I live in Brisbane, Australia and when I'm not writing, I can be found with a nice glass of wine and spends her time with her husband and holidaying with her three children. My favourite way to spend an evening is curled up on a couch next to my own hot alpha, reading and making the most of a quiet night in... well maybe not so quiet... if you read my books then you know what I mean.

More by J.F. Lowe

A Sailors Daughter

A forbidden love. A secret desire. A deadly past. A fight for survival.

At seventeen she made her oath to Queen and country, but nothing could have prepared her for life as a navy recruit. As Jenna steps onto the parade ground for the very first time, her life changes forever when she meets the tall, dark and handsome Petty Officer Rhys Morgan.

Faced with her first night legally as an adult and her eighteenth birthday, Jenna has only seconds to choose between the loneliness of the navy base or to trust the Petty Officer. She had no idea what will be asked of her or the boundaries that will he would push as he introduces her to his secret life.

Petty Officer Rhys Morgan hasn't been so attracted to a woman like this in years. His life at sea as a Petty Officer meant his relationships never lasted, like his first marriage. But the little recruit intrigues him like no other. Failing to be able to keep his distance as her instructor, the little recruit soon becomes all that he wants, needs, and craves.

This novel contains explicit sexual content, graphic language, and situations that some readers may find objectionable. Not intended for those under the age of 18.

Love Games

It's erotic, it's romantic, and wonderfully suspenseful. Hold on tight and get ready for a wild ride!

Married Games

Matthew Davidson was everything she'd ever dreamed of in a man and more. But two years after marrying the construction mogul, Sarah's fairytale romance falls apart taking them to a place of sex, lies, and murder. Sarah doesn't know whether she can trust the man she married... or even herself.

Revenge Games

After finding out that in her husband past he liked to share women with his best friend, Sarah realised that she knew nothing about the man she married. Now she is caught up in a game she didn't even know she was playing.

Sinful Games

It's been five years and yet the scars still show on my body. My husband Matthew still wakes with night terrors each night and they have only gotten worse since our beautiful daughter Katherine was born. I want my husband back, our marriage back and I'm willing to do anything to get it. Even if it means submitting to Matthew's deepest desires.

Connor

For all these years, I kept my love for Sarah a secret. After I stood beside Matthew as he married her, I thought I'd forever be a bridesmaid to love. But who would have thought one phone call could change it all. Second place doesn't cut it anymore, so when they say 'You can't have your cake and eat it too' well, I decided f#@k them. It's time I got my just desserts.

This novel contains explicit sexual content, graphic language, and situations that some readers may find objectionable. Not intended for those under the age of 18.

Subscribe

Subscribe to J.F. Lowe's newsletter and get the inside scoop on new and upcoming releases, marketing information, FREE BOOKS, sales, book signings, giveaways, and much more!

CLICK HERE

Review

If you enjoyed this book, please review it or recommend it to others so they can find it, too.

Wickedly Innocent

www.ingramcontent.com/pod-product-compliance
Lightning Source LLC
Chambersburg PA
CBHW072145130726
47909CB00004BB/1166